At Peace

Not In Pieces

Powering Through My Pain

At Peace

Not In Pieces

Powering Through My Pain

BY CHERISSA JACKSON

ISBN: 9780996794183

LCCN: 2016916663

Dedication

I dedicate this book to my beautiful daughters (Anita and Ashley) who make me proud to be a mother, a mentor, and counselor. Your greatest is Within you. Be bold, be fierce, be confident and never let FEAR hold you back. Spread your wings and soar like an eagle. I'm proud of you, and I love you dearly.

Table of Contents

Overview

I knew I always wanted to help people. As a kid, I would sacrifice myself to please others and feel good about myself. It was something about seeing the joy in someone's eyes when they felt that my actions were genuine. That is what inspired me. I didn't know that I would chase that feeling my entire childhood and adulthood. I recall a time when I needed school supplies for school and instead of asking my parents to purchase those items, I repaired the holes of my book bag, so my parents didn't have to spend money on another one. I remember feeling the sense of relief that I had granted them by not having to worry about what I needed. It was that feeling that I didn't understand nor could I articulate. Even today, I've been told that I have this "Savior" mentality and that I just want to save everyone. By no means will I or have I ever declared myself someone's "Savior" because I don't possess that power. Consequently, I do believe I can see the potential in everyone, and I only want to support, and assist them in achieving their goals in life.

Many relationships have developed in my life because I could always see someone's potential and their desire to be successful. From the moment the conversation starts, I would begin to decide if I could help them. My little TV antennas would burst out from my head and chime a ringtone, "I got you, I got you." At that moment, I'm sizing up the situation to see if I can help them excel and propel to the next level. I would never think of it as a potential romantic engagement. My objective would strictly be to evalaute a person's desires and needs and determining if I could tap into it and help them. I never reflected on the idea that I had always been sacrificing myself for others even to the detriment of my own emotional, psychological, and physical needs. I knew that I had the capability to survive without my needs being met, or at least that is what I thought. For so long my needs were placed on a shelf, collecting mounds of dust, spider webs, hidden behind other walks of my life and forgotten. I processed at a very young age that bringing joy to others would be my reward. That it would fill up my cup of loneliness, my longing for love, and the desire to allow myself to be loved. I had to decide what the best solution would be so I would no longer give so much without someone filling me up with joy, just as I had done for others for so many years.

At Peace is my journey to finding tranquility and serenity in my daily walk with disappointments, diagnosis with Post Traumatic Stress Disorder (PTSD), failures and successes. My life was so overwhelmed with internal misery and self-loathing until I realized I needed "Peace that surpassed" my understanding. I started on this journey to figure out how and why I got to this place and then developed a plan to get myself out quickly.

I remember feeling a sense of anxiousness on my journey to discovery and resurrection. I was ready for a change and I knew it could not be a marathon but a sprint to becoming better. I thought peace meant sitting at home, cell phone not ringing, not talking about a girlfriend or boyfriend drama, and just walking around not really focused on anything. Little did I know, that was not peace but misery. Who wants to sit at home alone in silence? Who doesn't want their phone ringing? If it's your loved ones, you would want to talk to them, right? I can't question the drama comment because still to this day, I don't like drama nor do I desire any drama in my life. But, the bottom line was I wasn't "At Peace", I was in a peaceful environment. I created a peaceful space in which to operate, but I wasn't creating a peaceful space for my heart, soul, and mind. It wasn't until the diagnosis of my PTSD that I began to understand why my actions and thoughts were the way they were.

Long before PTSD, I would crowd my schedule with daily activities, anything that wouldn't allow me to sit still and be with myself. I was afraid to be with myself so if I was busy I didn't have to do that at all. Just like after a storm, a rainbow will come, or the sun will peak through, my internal woes showed up. It was like a tsunami had come and destroyed my pretty glass house with stain glass windows, mahogany floors, and silk drapes. That facade of being a put together mother, friend, lover, daughter, and sister was all a lie. I was living a lie, sacrificing what little I had left of myself and walking in quicksand, only to have my head remain above ground. Then one day I was sitting still and weeping until there were no more tears. I said to myself that I wanted and needed peace. I had to get my control back. I got myself up off the floor, went into my bathroom, wiped the tears way, sprinkled water on my face, looked myself in the mirror and said, "No more." How many times have you looked into the mirror but really never stared into your own eyes, look at your own eye color, and really see yourself? That day I did just that and took a look in the mirror at myself. And when I dared to take that look I saw something beautiful, my own brown eyes. I saw my reflection, and I saw that I was great, a survivor, a warrior, a conqueror, a fighter and an achiever. The words just came darting at me, ricocheting and bouncing back onto me.

Before that experience, I was doing what I needed to do to survive and get the job done. I wasn't taking care of myself and seeing the awesome wonder that God had created. I started crying again because those words described how strong I was and would be. All those years, I was waiting for someone to sacrifice for me and save me, but that day, I stopped sacrificing myself and saved myself. That same joy and relief that I felt when I did it for others, I felt vibrating throughout every ounce of my being. Conquering and acquiring my peace had begun. I was claiming my power to be at peace and not broken into pieces. I was now on this journey to power through my pains and become who I was intended to be without regret, disbelief or fear.

My desire is that anyone who reads this book will read it in its entirety, and you receive your peace. I had and still have struggles like each of you, not only with post-traumatic stress disorder but also self-worth, self-honor and seeing how great I am at times. The intention of this book is not to treat or take your challenges away but to have you use the principles described in this book to help you discover your peace and create a new you that's worth more than anything you can buy.

I had to realize that I could no longer be that "sacrificial lamb" for others. I had to choose myself as my project and work it until completion. No one else could do it for me. No one can do it for you, but you have to have the inner wherewithal to do it. You are worth it. I was and am worth it. The principles in this book will allow you to breakthrough some vulnerabilities that you may have. I know that these principles helped me and if you need help, that's okay. *At Peace* will help you gain your truth about yourself. It will provide the guidance to acceptance and empowerment needed to get through any obstacle in your life. I remember when I was contemplating getting a divorce thirteen years ago, my mother said, "When you are fed up and tired of your current situation, you will make a firm decision and do what's best for you." I did exactly that and continued to use that affirmation in every situation that I can. *At Peace* will help you make the decision to turn your life around, speak your truth, take action to make the necessary changes to move forward and empower you to be courageous and walk a new normal that's uncomfortable but rewarding. *At Peace* will help you power through your pains and provide you with assistance to be great and unstoppable.

At Peace details my experiences through each of the principles: acknowledge, transition, perseverance, engage, accept, courage and empowerment. Each chapter will describe my journey through each of these principles. My hope is as you work through these principles that it resonates in your heart as you pursue your serenity.

At Peace will help you "acknowledge" your fears and pains, "transition" into a better space using therapy, resources and help along the way. You will "persevere" through those obstacles with a positive mentality staying "engaged" in the process. You will "accept" your new normal and not be afraid of the challenges and remain "courageous" and fearless. Lastly, you will be awakened and feel "empowered" because you have endured the process. You will become more hopeful for the future and more determined to live life to the fullest.

I'm so honored and privileged to be able to share my story with you. I am grateful for the opportunity to inspire, motivate and encourage each of you. No longer will you be shackled by your past experiences, medical conditions, hopelessness, and disappointments. No longer will you desire to be great, you will be great. No longer will your reflection in the mirror be an image of you feeling and believing you are unworthy of happiness and a better life. There is life, hope, success, prosperity, and joy within you. In time, you will be able to obtain it. Unlike shattered glass that can easily be swept up and discarded, you are not trash. Your broken pieces can be glued, taped, welded, or cemented back together. When you put in the work that's required, change will come. You would have powered through those pains and now you are new and whole again. You will no longer see the cracks and the lines from the brokenness, but you will see a smooth surface perfected by your tenacity to work through your pains to get to your breakthrough.

Cherissa Jackson

Journal Page

Chapter I: Acknowledge

Today is a gloomy day. Rain is imminent, and though I wish for a beautiful sunny day, this is what today brings. Like the weather which can sometimes be totally unpredictable, life will throw you a fast, slow, or curve ball. You may even strike out sometimes. What matters most is how you rebound from each pitch. ACKNOWLEDGING the things you have control over is step one. When you acknowledge, you give yourself permission to admit and accept events and emotions instead of camouflaging or hiding them. For many years, that's what I did. It was easy to put on a smiling face and perky attitude to cover up the hurt inside. My first acknowledgment was recognizing that my parents did the best they could with the resources and tools they had in their toolbox to prepare me for my future.

Growing up in a two-parent household with siblings and an extended family of grandparents, aunts and uncles, provided structure and discipline. Because we all lived in close proximity, it was not uncommon for the "village" to keep you in order. Oftentimes it was best that you remained on your best behavior because it would be a domino effect of punishment. If you got in trouble with your aunt, the other aunts would know, and they would then tell your grandparents who would then tell your parents. So it was best to just walk that straight and narrow line because it was not worth all the involvement which meant more chastisement and more anguish. My parents rooted my siblings and me in the Baptist church. I sung in the choir, attended regular Bible study and several church services throughout the week. We were all required to study hard, and our report cards should reflect us doing our best. So was a lot of emphases was placed on academics because my parents did not receive a high school education. They managed to parent six kids and were parental figures to several of my cousins. They worked hard at good paying jobs for years to support our family without a high school diploma. They knew how important it was to obtain a high school diploma, and they were determined that we all graduated and pursued college. Nothing made them more proud I think than seeing each of their kids graduate and today in our family room there are pictures of all of us in our high school caps and gowns.

Because my parents worked hard and worked long hours, we were often cared for by my wonderful grandmother. She requested her Folgers instant coffee throughout the day, her long hair braided neatly weekly, and to be picked up on time for Sunday school on Sundays. She was a beautiful soul who saw in me as a young girl who I would become one day. She saw an ambitious, motivated, and talented woman destined for greatness. I often would sit and study in her bedroom after school while she would sew quilts from old torn, tattered clothes. She would create masterpieces with her designs and beautiful patterns. I was studying in her bedroom after school while she was sewing a quilt, which she often did. She would take old clothes that we had outgrown, tear them into pieces and create beautifully patterned quilts. I would read out loud when she was around because she enjoyed it. She read the Bible faithfully but enjoyed me reading out loud. I would sit by the window until it became too dark to read. I would often not turn on the lights to save her electricity. When it got too dark, I would hear her say, "turn that light on baby." "Yes Ma'am," I would say, and I would continue to read, and she would continue to quilt. This particular day, I kept going over this one history assignment for a long period of time and I just couldn't get it. She heard me attempt so many different memory techniques to grasp the information then finally she said, "You know you've been repeating that same thing over and over, take a break and come back to it, you will get it when you come back." She saw that I was frustrated, annoyed and irritated. I did what she said and left the room then came back minutes later. Before I started back, she said, "You have to be patient with yourself and know that you will never be perfect. There is only one perfect man, and that is God, and baby you ain't him, so give yourself a break and stop beating yourself up!"

At that moment, I didn't truly understand what she was attempting to teach me. She was trying to convey that I needed to "acknowledge" my imperfections and accept that I will never be perfect.

I wish I had learned that lesson sooner than later because after high school and leaving home; I was left without guidance about life and what it would bring. I left home thinking that I would meet the perfect guy, have the perfect marriage, have the perfect kids, live in the perfect home and live happily ever after. Man, was I wrong. I wasn't prepared for the "buffoonery" that came to a gullible, unsure, sheltered little country girl. I believed in this fairy tale about life being kind and wonderful. The reason I felt this way was because I had no true role models to show me what love looked like or what a good man should be. So because I didn't have it, I created it for myself and failed miserably. I acknowledge that failure because very soon after leaving home and enlisting into the military, I fell in love or what I thought was love quickly. I wanted what I thought love should feel like. Immature and unknowing, I was smitten by a handsome, smooth talking guy that I later married and had beautiful daughters by. As I matured and grew older, I became wiser and discovered what I wanted and needed.

I had not failed at anything before so enduring a divorce was traumatic and unsettling for me. I was a great student in school, excelling in every aspect but was failing at being a wife. At that time, I didn't know what being a wife meant besides what I saw my Mother do for my Father. I cooked, cleaned the house, took care of the girls, went to work every day, I was loyal, faithful and submissive. I thought that this list of wifely duties should have worked because that is what I created in my mind. I completed the checklist. I did what was required of me or at least what I thought was required. No one ever taught me how to compromise, how to let a man be a man and be the head of the household. I did not know that you could still be independent and that my needs were important. I saw my Mother take care of all six of her children and the household while my father worked and financially ensured we had what was needed. Though my Mother worked, she remained submissive as to how the household and finances were managed. That was the "old school" mentality. Growing up seeing the "old school" way of being a wife, I didn't realize that was my parents' idea of being in a relationship. I thought that's how I needed to be as well. We mimic what we see, and that's exactly what I did.

With my failed marriage, I acknowledged that just like my parents did the best they could with the resources they had, I did the best I could with the knowledge I was given and had obtained along the way. I had to acknowledge that doing my best was not a failure, but a success. The divorce was very bitter, and though I wanted it to be amicable, we couldn't come to that point. I never thought two people who once loved each other or thought it was love could react so unkindly and heartless towards each other. The decision to divorce came after years of internal loneliness and despair. I knew walking down the aisle that the man waiting for me at the altar wasn't my prince charming. I had seen behavior that I now know today was unbecoming of the husband I wanted to spend the rest of my life with forever. I cried the entire time walking to him with my brother giving me away. I will never forget my brother noticing my distress and saying that I didn't have to do this and that we could turn around the stop the wedding. I said to him under my breath that I wanted to continue and that I didn't want to disappoint everyone that was there, nor did I want to disappoint my future husband who was standing at the altar. I wish I had the courage to do exactly that on that day. I was a coward, and I was afraid of disappointing others to the detriment of myself. Again, sacrificing myself for the good of others. We had some good years and some really awful ones. The greatest gift was having daughters that we co-parented, who have grown into wonderful young ladies. I grew from that experience. I acknowledged my dysfunction in the relationship and its demise.

When you acknowledge your mistakes and mishaps, you can then be accountable for your actions, take responsibility and move forward. What I discovered was that I'm a survivor to the core. I remember the day I decided I wasn't afraid of divorcing and accepting everything that came along with it like being single with twin daughters, etc. I was getting the girls ready for school, and they were leaving the house getting into the car, and I was following them. Their Dad and I had gotten into a verbal altercation, and the final words were, let's just get a divorce. I said yes, and I will contact a lawyer today. It was like a breath of fresh air had entered my soul. I had finally admitted out loud that I wanted out and needed to hear myself say it to move forward.

Then came my greatest "save me" moment. I went into survivor mode. Survivor mode is when you look at your situation realizing the difficulties ahead, but you still continue to march forward. I knew to survive the emotional and psychological battles that were waiting for me; I had to plan. I had to prepare myself to be a single parent. Check. I had been functioning like one already within the marriage. Then I had to prepare for the financial strains of having my own apartment, taking care of all the amenities alone, feeding, clothing, and paying for my daughter's education.

I knew I could work in the hospital as a nursing assistant until I passed my nursing boards. I had just finished Nursing School when this divorce issue drummed up for the fifteenth time, and I was leaving for my first deployment to Turkey. That time away solidified what I needed to do when I got back. So I acquired a nursing assistant job at a local hospital two minutes away from my new apartment to ensure I could support myself and the girls. I worked constantly. I was on active duty working for the Air Force during the day and worked at the local hospital pulling double shifts on the weekends. Thank goodness my oldest sister and parents didn't live too far from the girls and me. They would take care of them each weekend. I would meet my parents on Fridays, and my oldest sister would bring them home to me on Sundays.

Survivor mode allowed me to rebuild my finances from financial ruins after the divorce and prevented us from suffering any hardships. Though I was exhausted, my endurance and strength to handle that regimen for almost a year spoke to my tenacity, perseverance, and refusal to give up. While surviving, I didn't acknowledge these attributes. I felt as if I was doing what was required to move forward as a single parent. It wasn't until now that I recognize how tough those times were and how I made it through. What that experience taught me is that challenges will come in your life. My challenges were leaving home unprepared for life lessons of love, marriage, divorce, children, and single parenthood.

My path was like college. I had to learn along the way, and I'm still learning. As I'm learning, I'm accepting the things about myself that I cannot change. I ask for discernment and understanding for those things that I can, and lastly, I ask for the wisdom to know the difference. Soon after settling into my new life of single parenting, I had the desire to try love again. Some of the relationships were beautiful and brought me happiness for the moment while the others were disastrous.

The key was not allowing myself to give up. Each encounter was another lesson to teach me about myself in order to nurture the person I'm now becoming. I wasn't afraid of the experience, but I was afraid of the process and the aftermath. The process of getting to know someone and then discover they were not who I thought they were. Then dealing with the aftermath of the breakups and being dumped or doing the dumping was exhausting.

These were challenges for me because I believe we are attracted to people for different reasons. It was not always about obtaining a relationship; it could simply be for companionship, friendship or business. My test has always been picking which category each person should be in initially. Man, would I mess this up and probably the reason I suck at matching today. The person that should be a friend, I would put in the relationship category knowing he wasn't capable of a relationship. I would put someone in the friendship category when they were incapable of being a friend and just wanted to hang out now and then.

I had to acknowledge that it's okay to take my time and explore each person. There was no rush to decide which roles they would play in my life. Ultimately, I had to decide that life was too short to keep mismatching. This also included some of the friendships I've experienced. I have had friendships that have been very one sided. The person needed me more that I needed them, inundating me with their drama. I kept trying to save them from their woes while they overloaded me with all of their chaos. And most of the time they remained in their situation and never moved forward.

So, I ask you, what is important for you to acknowledge in your life? What will you accept? This is the first step to overcoming any obstacle in your life. Accepting its existence, looking at it square in the face and believing that you will endure, overcome and move forward. Accepting your truth about yourself and whatever you are facing will bring peace to your mind, body, and soul. The broken pieces from that ordeal will not even matter anymore. Now it's time to rebuild a new you. Besides acknowledging and accepting my divorce, disappointing relationships, flaws, and imperfections, I had to accept my diagnosis of post-traumatic stress disorder.

I have seen firsthand the PTSD symptoms challenging the soldiers while taking care of them in the combat hospitals. They suffered while on deployments and when they returned home to their families. Some suffered more than others, but they all had the common thread of memories that would not fade away. For so long I had compartmentalized my symptoms. I had packaged them into nice Tiffany boxes with a beautiful ribbon and hid them away. When the symptoms surfaced, I knew what it was, and I faced it. I didn't run from the diagnosis, even though I felt isolated and suffered alone. I knew that I would and could survive. I had to accept a diagnosis that had a stigma attached that said I wasn't good enough or less than others. Though I recognized the diagnosis, I refused to accept the negative connotations that came with it. I had survived going to war. How many people can say that today? I didn't allow the negativity to control me. I went into "Survivor Mode" again, reached out for help, did the work and surrendered to my new baseline, my new self. Although it was scary, I knew I had the strength to work through my painful memories and thoughts and become whatever I chose to become. So can you.

Chapter II: Transition

When I think of transitioning I think of a smooth, fluid motion from point A to point B. In life, everything has some form of transition. From a fetus to an embryo, to an infant and then to a toddler, life will transition. There is no stagnation in the evolution of life, and there is no stagnation when you acknowledge your hurt, pain, and diagnosis. And then you have to work through it all and transition out of it into a new space. When I transitioned out of my divorce, I was left with 3 "B's": brokenness, being broke, and bitterness. The feeling of brokenness was the most devastating of them all. I had given all of myself for life to say try again, or not now. I felt fooled and misled. I wasn't myself. I was unsure, uncertain, and couldn't understand how I could make such a mistake or fail so miserably. That brokenness led to many unfulfilled relationships that never evolved into anything permanent. I was searching for a way to mend the broken spirit that haunted me. I wanted that void filled and found the comforts of a man to be my anecdote.

Later I realized that remedy did nothing for me. If anything I sank deeper into the pit of brokenness and feeling sorry for myself. I hid it well. I had to put on a jovial personality around my children and at work, because that was the persona everyone knew. I was carrying a huge tumor inside that was infected with loneliness, heartbreak and worthlessness. When I realized my condition, I knew I needed to transition or make a change to get my life back. I had to conquer the fears that made me feel broken. I had to realize that I was not broken, but my thoughts about myself were shattered into millions of pieces. Those pieces of devastating thoughts were too much to bear at times, but I needed to work through the process and recognize the change that needed to occur to save me.

The second "B", being broke. I left the marriage broke and in financial ruins. I didn't care about the money and fighting over the finances because I wanted peace and I knew I wouldn't find it within the marriage. The saving grace that kept me afloat was the military and knowing that every two weeks I was getting paid. I lived from paycheck to paycheck. I ensured the girls had childcare, food, and clothing. I also ensured that we had electricity and a vehicle that operated safely. Everything else was beyond my means. I was thankful that I had a supportive family that would assist when needed. I appreciated that so much. I couldn't depend on the military and family to fix my financial hardship. I had to decide what changes and sacrifices could help get me through this turmoil. Working as a nursing assistant provided the relief that helped me transition out of the ruins. That experience taught me so much. Although I never lived beyond my means, it made me more aware of what being financially sound can do for you and made me very conscious and cautious about my investments.

The final "B", bitterness. I was bitter for a very long time. I was bitter at men, God, Cupid, the whole world actually. I couldn't understand how I could get dealt the wrong hand. I wondered what I did so wrong in my life that I had to go through all of this madness. Being bitter is hard work. I was never positive, I had no joy or happiness, I pretended to be someone I wasn't, it was exhausting. After months of feeling bitter and worn out from feeling cheated and fed up, I had to make a change. I had to transition out of being an unhappy person to finding my joy. It wasn't easy, but I had to do it. I had to recognize that life was too short, and I needed to be available and be a good role model for my daughters to follow. It wasn't easy because I had to become comfortable with who I was becoming. This person was new, and I had to understand my new found needs and desires. I had to decide what made me happy now. The change will always be uncomfortable because it's new and you have to get comfortable with it. You have to trust the process and remain optimistic that the change will work and yield the desires you want like joy, happiness, love, etc. There are no certainties with change, but you won't know what the outcome will be unless you try.

The day that I was commissioned as an officer in the Air Force, I could finally breathe. My finances were looking up, I had passed my nursing certification and was now a Registered Nurse and the Air Force decided to commission me as an officer. I had grown accustomed to being an enlisted member working on the flight line ordering parts for aircrafts. Now that I was an officer in the Air Force, I was held to a higher standard with more expectations. I was the epitome of a great leader, and I had to succumb to greater responsibilities. Now this transition was challenging. This change placed the girls and me in a better financial bracket, but it also meant that I was in charge of someone else's life. I will never forget my first assignment on a very busy medical, surgical unit and the assignment of 11 patients. My heart was racing, and I had to decide that day if I was going to sink or swim. I was the new kid on the block so I knew this assignment was a test to see how I would handle the pressure. Little did that charge nurse know that while I was in training, I requested to be challenged and given extra patients because I knew Wilford Hall where I was going to be assigned was a busy military hospital. So for the three months that I was in nursing training, I was preparing and planning for my transition to my new assignment on a busy unit at Wilford Hall Medical Center.

I wanted to master my skills while in training so that I would be the best nurse once I started the new unit. I figured if I could handle the extra patient load while in training where I could get tips from my preceptors and instructors that I would surely soar at my new assignment. When my 11 patients were assigned, I didn't grumble nor did I let the older nurses who I knew were watching me, see me sweat. I took the assignment with excitement for I had already developed a plan of attack while listening to reports from the night shift nurse. I remained poised and worked my strategic plan to get through that shift. My feet were tired; I was exhausted but at the end of the shift, I felt elated and excited about my accomplishment. I knew that if I could survive that day that I was ready for this new transition in my life. Before departing, one of the civilian nurses who had been on that unit for years came over to me and commented that I had done exceptionally well on my first day and that I was a great nurse to have on that unit. The lesson learned that day was that I embraced a new change. Instead of complaining and objecting to the assignment, I accepted it but remained confident in my abilities to complete the task.

Many times in life, we say what we are willing to do when the circumstance is not starring us in the face. When obstacles come, it's that will power to adjust and overcome the challenge that will get you through. That is when transitioning occurs. I had now transitioned from being a divorcee and broke to a commissioned officer and loving my new career as a nurse. As my career path was changing so was my desire to embark on relationships and search for love. The girls were older now, and I wanted to take a chance and see what Cupid would bring me. I was certain after years of working on my career, physical and psychological wellbeing that I was definitely ready for a relationship. Not! I tried to connect with men, but there remained voids in my life that I needed to fill for myself. Unknowingly, my expectations and needs had changed from what they were while married. I had not realized that I needed more until I allowed myself to commit to a four-year long-distance relationship. Subjecting myself to multiple trips to visit him brought that into perspective for me. I needed him to be available to me not only on the phone, via text message, or by showering me with gifts. I needed him physically and emotionally; I needed the support that I was giving him while he was building his business.

Those four years were a constant emotional roller coaster because a part of me wanted the idea of having a partner but because it was long distance, it really wasn't a partnership in my eyes. After multiple attempts and even an engagement, I knew the relationship wasn't going to have any longevity. I had to leave that relationship knowing that I still had more to learn about myself. I still needed to discover what my needs, wants, expectations, deal breakers, and my willingness to compromise if I needed to, looked like. I saw a change in me. I saw a maturity brewing. I saw myself blossoming like a beautiful flower. I knew as this change was occurring that I was growing as a mother. My greatest joy was and still is being a mother. I wanted to ensure my changes and sacrifices were all to benefit my daughters. They would see me being strong and driven. They would see me striving to live a successful life. They would understand what hard work really was and how not to run from it. As I transitioned, I lost friends that didn't understand why I did not want to do the same things they were doing. I lost acquaintances because now I was no longer willing to listen to their drama and be a part of their pity party. I had to make a decision for myself. I had to decide what was important to me, and that was my focus.

What will be your reason to make a change? Will it be a bad relationship? Will it be getting yourself out of financial ruins? Will it be changing your career to inspire yourself and others around you? Whatever you decide, the first step is making a decision to transition. Yes, unless you prepare yourself, it will not be easy. So, prepare yourself. Do whatever is required to get yourself where you want to be. Whatever it took for me to prepare for the change, I did it almost mechanically. After you have done the necessary preparation, you then have to move past the fear of the unknown. The change will be new, and unless you have a crystal ball, you can only hope and wish for a successful outcome. In the meantime, you can't let the uncertainty of the outcome deter you. You have to stay on track and remain optimistic. There is no room for negativity while transitioning. You have to remain positive and determined to make it to the finish line. Many times while making some horrible choices throughout my journey, those mishaps only prepared me for the bumps in the road. Or like we would say in the South, the roadkill. Use every opportunity you have to increase your tools in your toolbox of success. No experience is wasted. You are destined for success and prosperity. What will you do to achieve it?

I had a personal trainer once, and I remember him saying to me whenever I wanted to stop or give up, "How bad do you want it?" At the time I was sweating, in pain and my entire body was fatigued, so I could not respond. At that moment, I couldn't answer that question. It would be a day or two later when I would hear him in my head, and I decided to try and answer his question. How bad did I want to be in shape and be in the best shape of my life? At what cost was I willing to put into the training to achieve the desired outcome that I was looking for? My answers were always, "because I can, and I will do what I've sought out to do." I will not give up or abort the mission that I had set for myself. Aborting or giving up was a sign of failure. I was determined not to fail based on being a little fatigued or out of shape. Soon afterwards when he would ask me that question during a session, I would say, "Real Bad!" He would chuckle, and I would continue working out giving each session 100% of my time and effort. So I'm asking you, "How bad do you want it." Will you accept the challenge of change and want it "Real bad" to do something about it? You can do it. You must do it. You must tackle change like your life depends on it. And honestly, your life does depend on it because you will remain in the same position if you don't. Next time you are up against the most challenging obstacle in your life ask yourself and answer the question, "How bad do you want it!"

Chapter III: Perseverance

When I think of perseverance, I think about all the things that I had to endure and go through in life. We don't all share the same challenges or obstacles. However, it is how we choose to overcome those experiences that determine our fate. Perseverance is the ability to do something despite difficulty or delay while achieving success. It's that course of action, that purpose, and that drive within you, that causes you to work harder to achieve your goals. Failure is not an option when you strive to persevere. Failure is a hindrance if you're trying to persevere through any difficult situation. When you persevere, success is on the horizon. Success is the only thing that you think about, and you know that it's going to be waiting for you at the finish line. When you persevere, you have to know that you are capable and ready to fight a fight that you never had to fight before. You have to be prepared and know that there will be obstacles, hurdles, and mishaps along the way. It's that drive and determination that allows you to persevere and overcome. In my life, I've had many challenges that I've had to persevere in order to become the person I am today.

One challenge, in particular, was to complete nursing school while on active duty, raising school age daughters and survive a tumultuous marriage. It took drive and determination for me to overcome this challenge. I knew it was an uphill battle, having to work the night shift for the military then attending nursing school afterwards then putting on a wife and mother's hat in order to take care my kids and my husband at the time. Many days I wanted to quit. I remember a time when I was so tired from this constant routine; it had been several months, and I actually fell asleep at the wheel. I was only a block away from the house, and I accidentally drifted off and fell asleep. By the time I woke up, I had plunged into the back of a pickup truck. Thank God no one was injured. Even though both vehicles were barely scratched, this accident showed me that I needed to make some changes in my life in order to be safe.

The changes I made included making sure I got to sleep after my daughters went to bed at night. On the weekends, I tried to complete as many household tasks as I could. I would do laundry, clean the house, and spend time with the family. By doing so, throughout the week I had time to study and catch a nap before starting my night shift with the military. That schedule continued for two years until I completed nursing school. I learned many lessons from that experience. I learned that I could accomplish anything I put my mind to. I learned that once you set a goal nothing, and no one can, or will deter you from achieving that goal. It did not matter how tired I was, how many arguments went on in the household, the homework assignments and activities that the girls had throughout the week, or my duties as a non-commissioned officer in the military, I was determined to complete nursing school. There were so many times that I thought I would never complete the program. I had difficulties learning the material because I was fatigued and many times I did not have time to complete assignments. I remember being in my counselor's office several times a semester about complaints from instructors that I was nodding off in class, not participating, and being inattentive. My counselor told me that many instructors did not believe that I could or would complete the program. I was told that I needed to remove some of my responsibilities and to make nursing school my priority. I would tell my counselor all about my daily routine and the responsibilities I had. Although she was sympathetic and empathetic, she was also not convinced that I would complete the program. I studied as hard as I could and many times barely making the mark that was required to continue in the program. I saw this as a success while many saw this as merely getting by.

It seemed like each semester became more difficult and instead of receiving support from my spouse at the time, the military, and the school of nursing, I felt like I was on my own and that everyone was expecting me to fail. I remember one particular instructor; she was considered the hardest and meanness instructor at the school of nursing. This instructor was definitely out to get me. By this time everyone in the program knew who I was and my challenges. This instructor insisted that I sit on the front row of her class and repeatedly would ask me questions to ensure that I was prepared for class. Many times, she would ask that I stay afterwards and talk to her about how I was feeling and dealing with the pressure. I will never forget the day she said to me, you will not make it through this program. She continued to say that she did not believe I would be a good nurse and that it was best that I choose another career that didn't require as much time as nursing school. This instructor haunted me for the entire semester. I believe she wanted to see if I would break. I believe she wanted me to fail so that she could tell me, I told you so. She did not realize that I had the tenacity and the ability to persevere and overcome. What she didn't know was that I knew within every ounce of my being, that I was destined to be a nurse, and she nor anyone else would stop me. What she and others didn't realize was that I was taught early in my childhood to never be a quitter. I was taught that when things got tough, there were two choices you can make. You can choose the path that was easy, quitting; or you could choose the path of pushing through no matter how long it took in order to complete a task.

Though I felt like I was in quicksand, praying and hoping and wishing to be that stellar student, I had to accept that given my circumstance; I had nothing to prove to anyone, and the goal was just to finish the program and be a success story. Because of my schedule, I didn't participate in any of the activities surrounding the University nor did I have time to hang out with my classmates. Every minute counted in my schedule. I knew when I started; it would not be easy. I knew I would have an uphill battle. I knew I would not have the support. I knew the odds were stacked against me. But like many things that soon followed, I persevered. I turned a negative into a positive, and I studied harder, was more determined, and kept my eyes on the prize. I didn't care what people thought. I didn't care who supported me. I knew it was me against the world. I learned during that experience that sometimes you have to fight alone. For two years, I fought alone and in silence. I walked the walk every day, knowing that I was fighting to the death until graduation day.

Those two years are a blur to me at times. It seemed like those years passed by quickly. What I remember most, was attending the candlelit ceremony for our graduation. I would never forget that on the front row of the Cathedral was that one instructor who did not believe I would finish the program. When I came on stage to light the candle, I looked up, and our eyes met. She nodded and gave me a small grin as if to say she approved. At that moment, I saw the good in all the wrong I thought she had done. Perhaps she saw the drive in me, and she wanted to push me knowing that I could take the criticism. Perhaps she wanted to see if I would quit. Nevertheless, when I walked off the stage, I exhaled a sigh of relief. Lighting the candle confirmed that I had the willpower to overcome the obstacles. Lighting the candle was a rebirth and an understanding of how strong I really was and could be. Later that night after the celebration with family and friends and I had a moment alone, I cried, not because I was sad but because I was rejoicing in what I had accomplished. I knew that day that I could be an inspiration to someone else who thought that they weren't good enough or wanted to quit.

Recently, I received a Facebook request from a fellow coworker who had worked with me during the time that I was in nursing school. At first, I did not remember her face. Later as she described where she worked and some of our conversations, I connected the name and face. She said to me, I remember l would always see you studying or with your daughters. She continued by saying you would always say you were going to finish nursing school come hell or high water. She stated that she watched in amazement for two years as I brought my books to work and found quiet time to study - all while being a good supervisor. She also mentioned that she recalled seeing me out with my daughters and the commitment I had to them inspired her. In the midst of those two years, I never thought or had time to think about how people perceived me during that time. My focus was completing nursing school and doing my best as a parent and spouse. It was great hearing that I was an inspiration to her because I would've wanted to have had someone to inspire me during that time. I believe that the trial I had in completing nursing school was a blessing to her and others who witnessed my struggle. To hear that I was an inspiration to her after so many years, made the difficult times worth it. She said, seeing my daily fight later inspired her to study hard as a single parent in order to attend college also. She also had to persevere in order to get the job done. It is not easy to remain consistent and disciplined when you're tired or feel like giving up. But you have to. No one has the same goals as you, so if you want to complete those goals, you have to dig deep down inside and find your inner strength and belief in yourself to push through the hard times. Even when no one else believes in you, you have to believe in yourself.

I thought completing nursing school was difficult, but being a single parent was another ballgame. Unlike nursing school which was a choice I made in order to better myself, being a single parent was my priority. It was my duty and my responsibility to be the best mother I could be. When the divorce was final, and my new life had settled in, I had to tap once again into "survival mode". I recall sitting still on a Monday and actually visualizing how I would be a single parent. That's what I would often do in survival mode. I would make a mental game plan in order to ensure I would cover every aspect of the ordeal. I would also have a backup plan; A, B, and C. I had a plan in case the girls got sick at school or if there was an emergency at school, if I woke up late for work, or arrived late to pick the girls up from daycare.

In survival mode, you have to cover every turn. I had to always be prepared as a single parent to do everything solo. I looked at this challenge and knew just like nursing school; I would persevere. As a single parent, my focus was my daughters and many times I had to put my emotions and wants on the back burner. I watched and was attentive to the girls as they transitioned from childhood to puberty. Having to be emotionally and psychologically available to teenagers with their hormonal changes was overwhelming. However, I knew this was the card that I was dealt; I could not change. As the girls grew older, it became easier because they were responsible and could take care of themselves. As the girls became more independent, we now had more free time to have fun and enjoy each other. I could see them growing and becoming beautiful young ladies. I could see that the many years of preparation was paying off. You see, as a single parent, the girls had to endure multiple school changes, meeting new friends, and adapting to new locations. The girls became independent at a very early age and were mature enough to stay home alone. They completed chores including laundry, cooking and cleaning the house. At the time, the girls saw doing these chores as fun times. They knew they were helping me as they saw me work long hours at the hospital. They wanted to make things easier for me as a single parent because they saw all the hard work I was doing to sustain the household. Often I felt guilty that the girls missed out on certain opportunities because I was the only one responsible for them. Many times I felt guilty about trying to enjoy my life because I felt their lives were more important and that they should have a wonderful childhood. No one gave me a handbook on how to be a single mother. I did the best that I could to instill good morals and values into my girls.

I believe persevering through single parenthood until my daughters became adults was the biggest challenge I've ever had. I was my own cheerleader. I knew I wanted to be a good role model for them. I knew that if they weren't successful, I would be the blame. I knew that if they had not stayed on the straight and narrow path, it would be because of the stigma of being a single parent. Like all other odds, this was another opportunity to defeat the odds. I knew within me that all the teachings that my parents had taught me and what I'd seen from them as they parented six children, that I could be a great parent. Because I refused to succumb to the plight of a single parent, I persevered through the odds. I trusted my abilities, I refused to be defeated, though I saw the challenges; I remained optimistic and hopeful for a good outcome.

As a single parent, you just never know how your kids will react to a difficult circumstance or mishap in their lives. I recall an event in which my daughter handled a situation with poise and grace. Today was one of those days that I got to see how one of my daughters would respond to an event in her life that was very unfortunate. She received the unfortunate information with poise and grace. We both knew the decision she was waiting on was imminent. As she spoke about the mishap, she was in a good place. She was not weeping or sobbing about the decision, nor was she willing to waddle in the what if's of the decision. I watched her dissect the decision which would impact her life with courage and fortitude. I saw my daughter turn into a warrior. She was now fighting for her future and her destiny to become what she sought after. I saw the determination in her face, and I heard how she would and could persevere through this obstacle. My daughter, like myself so many times, went into survivor mode. She began planning, researching, collecting data, and making calls to get all her questions answered so that she can make her next move. She was about her business. She did not let the unfortunate outcome deter her from her future. I was so proud to see that she could do this on her own. I was happy that she could embrace the lessons learned throughout this ordeal and push through to get the success she deserves. It was great to see that she could adapt and devise a strategy to overcome her situation. Again, its survival of the fittest.

You can either sit, cry and feel sorry for yourself about your circumstances, or you can push through, persevere, take life as it comes, and bust a move. That's one of the common sayings that I would say to my friends and family when they present a situation to me. I would say to them, are you ready to bust a move. Busting a move means you're ready to get up, take the bull by the horns and figure out a different plan in order to get the outcome you want. Busting a move means that you have to have courage within in order to pick yourself up out of the pitfalls of disappointment. Busting a move means you have to be able to shake off the negativity and find positivity in your situation. My daughter had a bust a move moment. I saw her determination to find a solution to her problem. Nothing could stop her. She refused to be defeated. These are all characteristics of someone who will persevere in life. I believe that because she has seen me work through countless problems and overcame so many mishaps that she has this innate ability to do the same. Man, what a great opportunity to see your child grow and mature. As I've always said, being able to overcome obstacles, or persevere, is something that is internal. Yes, you can learn how to be motivated and stimulated to get a job done. However, to have the internal drive and determination without assistance, says that you are your own motivator. Being your own motivator means that without a shadow of a doubt, with or without support, you can get through any obstacle in your life. I feel blessed and honored to have witnessed my daughter work through her problem and is now on the right track to obtaining and receiving what she wants to accomplish.

Little did I know coming into the military that I would be deployed multiple times. Getting the news of having to leave my daughters and go to war was one of the most devastating moments of my life. It was the unknown that had me anxious and uncertain. There were many things that needed to be done in preparation for the deployments. I wasn't concerned about my well-being because I was concerned about the girls. They would need to be transferred to another school, make new friends, adjust to a different household and worry about me while I was gone. I tried to prepare them as much as possible for this situation. As the months shortened to weeks, and weeks into the days closer to my departure, I could see how this transition was affecting them. I tried to console them as much as possible. I assured them, even though I didn't know myself, that I would return safely within the timeframe I was given. I prepared them for the holidays, birthdays, school events and our regular daily lives that we would miss together as much as possible. We did talk while

I was on deployment. We Skyped, wrote emails and letters to each other to ensure we stayed in communication.

Those were the most difficult times. For I knew I was no longer in control and that I could do nothing from Iraq and Afghanistan. I knew the girls were safe, but I wasn't there to wipe their tears away, hold their hands, or console their hearts as they waited for my return. We did an amazing job through all of those deployments. We remained consistent with our communication, and we were determined to lift each other until we reconnected. You see being deployed is not like taking a vacation for a few days and leaving your kids with their grandparents. When you are in a war, your mind has to stay focused on your safety and surviving. You have to remain vigilant at all times so that you would not put yourself in harm's way so that you can return home to your family and friends. Working long hours and never knowing when the enemy would attack, would often keep me very unsettled and unsure. Many emotions would come to mind including wondering if your children would still love you when you returned. Emotions like wondering if you were a good parent or a good friend or good sibling would arise. There were many moments during deployment where not only were you physically exhausted but psychologically exhausted. Particularly when you would receive no mail or correspondence from family and friends. It made you wonder did they care and if you really mattered. So not only did I have to persevere through the emotional detachment from my daughters but also from the emotional attachment to the soldiers I took care of each day. While busy taking care of the soldiers, you didn't have time to think about your family and the things happening back home. Those thoughts and memories would come as you were walking back to your bunker or attempting to sleep through the rocket attacks. Now I had to persevere through my thoughts.

Being deployed took me away from reality. The reality of parenting, paying bills, driving in traffic, and hanging out with friends. My new reality was waking up, getting something to eat, going to the gym, and working. That routine was now my new life. After several months, I became acclimated to war and what it took to survive in a combat zone. As the deployments were ending, I had to transition back to a life that was on hold for several months. Not only was this a scary feeling but also a sense of excitement. The instant joy of seeing your family is short-lived because you now have to jump back to all the duties and tasks you were responsible for before the deployments. Oftentimes it would be hard to rekindle relationships that you had prior to deployments. I had to decompress in order to get back to being a single mom, friend, sibling, and coworker. While friends and family are so excited to have you back home safe and are ready to get back to how things were, for me, it would be more difficult.

With each deployment, it became more and more difficult for me to adjust back to my routine once I returned home. But I had to persevere through all those emotional and psychological pitfalls that had laid dormant until my return. I had to understand that the things that I missed, I could never get back. The birthdays, celebrations, holidays and the events would not be in my memory bank. They would be other people's memories. I had to get over that. I had a job to do, and I completed the job and returned home. I had to face the fact that everyone had changed including myself. I had to accept that change was inevitable. I was no longer in control because there were others influencing my circle. I had to forgive myself for believing I was not needed or wanted when I got back. My only concern with being deployed was never whether or not I would survive but more so who would I become after the experience. Each deployment I came back different, that's normal, how could I not. Though I went four times, I was never troubled by location, preparation, or countless processes. My biggest concern was how it would affect my children and my family. I'm proud to say we overcame and persevered through the separation and our bond actually became stronger throughout the deployment. You see sometimes you have to go through some challenges in order to see a change so that you can move forward. And that is what overcoming is all about, getting into survival mode, busting a move, and moving forward. I'm so thankful for those who stuck through it with me. If it wasn't for them, I don't believe I would have the state of mind that I do now. I feel so blessed to not only come back without injuries but to know I had support throughout the deployments was remarkable.

One important aspect needed in order to persevere is the ability to acknowledge your role in any failures that have occurred. No one likes to fail, but failing is just another opportunity for you to succeed. Failing is a second chance to complete what you didn't the first time. Failing is the universe's way of saying not yet or not now, but try again. When you acknowledge your part in the mishap, you can use that as a lesson and a guide of what not to do again. Taking ownership and accepting your responsibility about what happened will motivate you to try harder. I know this principle well. I am the type that chooses not to sit and have a pity party when I fail at anything. I might cry and feel disappointed, but then I know that life goes on. I then go into my Olivia Pope mode and try and find a solution to my problem. Jumping into this mode too quickly can be disadvantageous. If you don't ask yourself the questions of how and why you failed, you will not be able to prevent this mishap again. I had to learn that it's important to process the failure and include that process in my success. At first, I didn't do this, and it cost multiple attempts before succeeding. I believed that I wore an "S" on my chest and was superwoman. I was a single mother with great daughters that I was parenting alone, I had completed nursing school while working night shift on active duty, rebounded from financial ruins, returned safely from multiple deployments and my military career was progressing. How could I not be SUPERWOMAN? Well, my attempt at attending nurse anesthesia school as a full-time student and full-time active mother whose daughters were now in High school, was my kryptonite. In the first semester, I knew I was in over my head in trying to do what I had done to complete nursing school. I did not take the time to analyze the difference between the two circumstances. In nursing school, though going through a divorce, their father was there to assist, and the girls were five years old when I started. Attempting Certified Registered Nurse Anesthetist (CRNA) School when the girls were 15 years old was totally different. They were active in high school, and we did everything together. I didn't take the time to assess why I succeeded in nursing school or the failures during that time. Because I had succeeded before, that was all I was focused on. I did it, and I would do it again. Wrong! Had I processed the facts, I would have seen how impossible the attempt at CRNA was at that time in my life. I would have seen the impact it would have on the girls. I would have seen how to prevent the failed attempt. Because I didn't and because I was holding on to what I had done previously, I endured two miserably difficult semesters in CRNA School. I knew that I was drowning, but I wanted to prove everyone wrong; I had been accepted on my first attempt which is very uncommon, and I was holding on to the hope that I could tap into whatever I had done prior in nursing school to help me through. Needless to say, it never kicked in.

My daughters missed me because I was studying at the library all the time, getting home late and leaving early in the morning for work. I was missing seeing them grow up because I was so focused on myself. I was miserable in school because unlike nursing school, giving anesthesia wasn't fun to me and I couldn't get excited about it. I had to motivate myself to enjoy each class. Finally, after a long heart to heart conversation with a great friend, and diving into my acceptance and acknowledgment of how unhappy I was, I decided to withdraw from CRNA School. It was such a sigh of relief when I drove away from the campus and saw it in my rearview mirror. Later, I asked myself what I had done. Then the thoughts of me failing started to creep in. Failing is when you don't complete a task. I didn't finish so I had failed. That was such a tug on my heart back then that it took me months before I could talk about it. The revelation that came was that I was suffering in silence about the ordeal. When I started talking about it, I saw a new perspective. I was awakened from the failure to see how to persevere through it and use my story to help others. As I told friends and family about my defeat, it no longer became a story of failure but a story of how to overcome. Talking about it and not being ashamed of the defeat was helping me to see how powerful I was to throw the towel in and choose my family and sanity over being unhappy and miserable. I endured, I persevered!

I used that experience to help me find my passion to become an entrepreneur and business owner. I now know to examine every detail before making a decision because of that situation. I had to learn that lesson. That is what failures will do. They will teach you a lesson. In the end, it's up to you to remember that lesson and to follow through. It's okay to take a breather and gather your thoughts before moving into another adventure. It's almost imperative that you do. Regrouping and processing is a sure way of knowing you are persevering through that situation. Now your mind is free, and before you initiate plan B, you can be certain of what not to do the next time. In the end, I needed to learn that lesson of failure because had I not, I would be continuing down the path of wanting to do the impossible without thinking about the risks. Everything you do in life has a risk. You can risk it all and fail, or you can risk it all and succeed. Either way, you have to be prepared for both. You also have to be ready for the consequences that will follow.

My challenges with PTSD (Post-traumatic stress disorder) showed me that I could also persevere through my obstacles. When I was diagnosed with post-traumatic stress disorder, I was not shocked by the diagnosis. I had seen the disorder and treated many soldiers with the disorder many times. Because of my insomnia, hyper-vigilance, depression, hopelessness, isolation, and hyper-alertness, I knew that I was in trouble. I hid my symptoms for a long time, not only from my coworkers but also from my family. I did not want to be scrutinized or stigmatized by my disorder. I had to believe that I could and would deal with my situation and overcome it like I had done so many times before. My concern was that my PTSD did not look like anyone else's PTSD. So because my symptoms appeared less severe, I didn't want to mention my condition. It wasn't until I had to deal with my emotions after my daughters left for college that I knew I was in trouble. All of the emotions that I had compartmentalized for years came tumbling down. I didn't know how to deal with these feelings nor did I know who to discuss my vulnerabilities with. It wasn't until I decided that I wanted to become better that I took the next step; not only for myself but also as a mother, a friend, and a family member. I decided for myself that I was strong, wise and would persevere through these challenges. It wasn't easy at all.

Many times I felt like I was in this quicksand of emotions and uncertainties. I would often ask myself the question, "Would I ever snap out of it?" It was concerning when all I wanted to do was go to work, then come home. I didn't want to socialize, and I felt like isolating myself kept my secret alive. I soon discovered that this was not a healthy way to overcome and deal with my condition. In order to persevere and overcome, I had to ask for help. Asking for help is not a sign of weakness. I didn't realize that until I actually sat and spoke with the therapist to explore my emotions and to deal with my symptoms. Instead of feeling weak, I actually felt empowered and stronger. I felt like I was wiser and equipped to confront all of my challenges and meet them head on.

Once I received help and worked through the process of understanding and improving my posttraumatic stress, I wanted to help others. I wanted others to understand how powerful they are because I had no one to tell me how powerful I was. I wanted to ensure that anyone dealing with PTSD was not suffering in silence, misdiagnosis, or left behind to deal with their symptoms alone. I wanted everyone to know that my focus is to help save and improve the lives of those suffering. Not on my watch would someone feel unsupported or left behind. I wanted everyone to see that even when faced with a mental disorder you still have the power to overcome. It takes being strong-willed, unstoppable, and having the desire to become better in order to move and push through obstacles.

Persevering is a choice. You can choose to become better. Then it is up to you to do what's required to become better. How you choose to overcome obstacles may be totally different than how I chose to overcome my obstacles. No two people are alike. We may all share some of the same stories and obstacles, but how we overcome them and choose to overcome them is different.

I remember the old cliché when life gives you lemons you make lemonade. That is how I choose to live my life. Each day I wake up hoping for a day free of challenges, obstacles or mishaps. Some days that's the case, other days not so much. And on those days when mishaps occur, I would find a way to turn the obstacle into a lesson learned or make lemonade. How do you know that you are persevering? You know when you are able to wake up each day with the new perspective, optimism, and the determination to plow through the storms in your life. When you can believe and trust that the day will be better than the day before that's how you know you are overcoming. I overcame a divorce, difficult times in nursing school, single parenthood, withdrawing from a graduate program, multiple deployments, and challenges of post- traumatic stress with bumps and bruises and scars that showcase that I am a survivor. I would hide my scars because I didn't want to appear weak or vulnerable.

I no longer choose to hide those scars because it reminds me of when life tried to break me but failed. You see, your scars tell a story, and your story will not be the same as anyone else's story. You have to acknowledge each chapter in your story to understand and see how you have defeated the odds, and you are now a living witness that you can overcome. When you persevere, you will find that you will be at peace and not broken into pieces. You must believe in your abilities and your innermost strength to move past your obstacles. You are the only one who will stand in your way. Only you know what you are truly capable of. You have to decide for yourself how you will overcome and in the words of my old personal trainer, how bad do you want it!

Chapter IV: Engage

I was once engaged to be married after a four-year relationship. Because it was a long distance relationship, I wondered where we would go from here. It was a waiting game now. What will we do differently than what we had already done before? Yes, of course, preparations for a wedding and everything that comes along with that was required. But what did it really mean to be engaged and to stay engaged? Now that that relationship is in the past, and I've since moved on, I truly understand the meaning of what being engaged is all about. When you're engaged, not in the sense of marriage, it means that something occupies your attention and secures your efforts. In other words, that means something grabs your attention to the point where nothing else matters. You are totally focused on that one thing, and every ounce of you is engulfed into that one thing. Being engaged and focused is pivotal to understanding who you are. When you are passionate about a person, place or thing, your mind is set on that person, place or thing. You are captivated by it. It is essential that you pin-point those things that keep you engaged. Determining those things will allow you to understand what is of priority to you and how supportive you can be to it. One of the things that I continue to stay focused on is my self-improvement. I'm constantly doing a self-checkup to decide and determine if I'm applying myself and giving my all to become a better person.

Analyze those things that have priority each day. Sometimes it's the business, sometimes it's the nonprofit, sometimes it's my relationships, sometimes it's just me taking care of myself. I do the self-checkups because I want to ensure that I engage wholeheartedly every ounce of myself into that one thing. Giving my all and giving 100% brings me closer to success. If I can't give it 100%, then I choose to disengage until I can. There are several areas that I believe you should stay engaged in. Here's my list: self-awareness, self-improvement, helping others, and knowing what's worth engaging. We will first take a look at self-awareness.

One day I posted on Facebook, "today, speak your truth without reservations or justification. You matter, and if you don't speak your truth and compromise, you will diminish who you are. We don't live in order to suppress our greatness in order for others to feel greater about themselves.   We live to love, support, care, and live life to the fullest." That post was all about self-awareness and staying engaged in who you are in order to be able to speak your truth and not compromise yourself for the sake of others. Oftentimes we forget that we are the precious gems we are. We forget in order to be the best for others we have to take care of ourselves. It wasn't until after the engagement dissolved that I began "checking" myself. Just like you check a piece of fruit in the produce section for bruises, rottenness, and insects, you have to "check" yourself also. I had to look myself in the mirror to acknowledge those bruises and scars from past experiences and realize that they didn't define me. When I looked in the mirror, I looked deep into my eyes and wanted to hide and camouflage my pains. However, when I "Checked" myself, I looked deep into my eyes and accepted those scars and called them out.... The stretch marks from multiple detours in unloving relationships, the sagging arms from the lack of motivation to improve myself, the unmanicured nails from feeling unworthy and unkept because I didn't matter, the list goes on and on. As I did the head to toe assessment calling out my imperfections and relating them to my life's misfortunes, I became more aware of how God made me. At one point, and I'm still a little shy, I hated taking pictures. What I saw in pictures wasn't what I saw in the mirror. But as I started "checking" myself, I began seeing that both images were the same. That was a revelation for me. The beauty I saw in front of me in the mirror was the beauty I saw in pictures, flaws and all. Instead of hiding them, I accepted them. Instead of masking them, I embraced them and revealed them. Instead of wanting to change, I embraced my condition and decided how I would cope moving forward. Self-awareness is that one "check" you must do to truly engage in your life and your passion.

What would you say you know most about yourself? Not just your favorite color, music, or past time. Here are a couple of things I know for certain about myself and I am aware of them at all times. I'm caring, thoughtful, and very supportive of everyone in my life. I know that I love hard and open my heart only to those that have earned my love and trust. I know that I'm destined for greatness and that nothing I've experienced was a mistake but my fate. I know that each day affords me a new opportunity to start anew and begin again. I know that the reason I've overcome obstacles is because of my faith and tenacity to be a survivor. I know that my hopes and dreams are obtainable with hard work and determination. To know yourself is crucial because when you need to inspire and motivate yourself, you have to know yourself in order to tap into what you need. When I'm in need of motivation and inspiration, I tap into my past experiences and use them as a roadmap to getting me back on track. I ask myself, how did you do that? It's like an "ah-ha" moment. Once I answer that question, I then apply it to that situation. It works for me. Knowing myself has allowed me to be aware of my happiness. Being happy meant knowing my needs, wants, and desires. Happiness starts from within. I don't look for someone or something to make me happy. People and things can only enhance my happiness. What makes me happy is not compromising for my happiness. Lord knows I've done enough compromising in my past. I've compromised self-love, self-awareness, and self-dignity for the sake of being happy. I've had to learn how and when to compromise for my happiness. I had to learn how to play in other's sandboxes and commingle without sacrificing myself. When you are self-aware, you know what makes you happy with or without others. I know that my happiness is rooted in my passions. I'm passionate about many things: advocating for Veterans with PTSD, helping others see their greatness, exposing my vulnerabilities in order to encourage and motivate others, and believing we all can support each other's endeavors without envy. Being passionate will drive your efforts and keep you going. It's nothing like having a mediocre day, not feeling motivated and then you get an opportunity to inspire others. I get fired up when I'm able to use my gifts and passions to see lives transform. I believe if I can help one person, my purpose in life has been fulfilled. Passion gives me life and encouragement to try harder and never get deterred, or side tracked from my desires. Passion helps me stay aware of my happiness and prevents me from compromising too much of myself. Self-awareness is the first step to engaging in your life's journey to be your best self.

Self-Improvement is next. Once you become aware, you now need to be prepared to do the work to self-improve. I detest when I talk to colleagues, and they talk about wanting to self-improve but are unwilling to do what's necessary to make the changes. Self-improvement is important, particularly when you become a CEO and want to advance your business. As the CEO of Jackson & Associates Legal Nurse Consultants, LLC and PTSFaces.TV, it was important for me to always look for opportunities to grow as an entrepreneur. I'm constantly looking for seminars, workshops, training, and conferences to attend to increase my knowledge. Self-improvement requires learning and embracing new ideas. I'm like a sponge, and I want to have as many tools in my toolbox to prepare and advance me to the next level. You have to be willing to put in the work to self-improve. You have to engage in all aspects of the process in order to embrace the fulfillment of improving. I was asked to attend a conference for young entrepreneurs with breakout sessions about pitching your ideas, raising capital, and collaborating with like-minded CEOs. I was scared to attend because the rostered appeared to have businesses that had been in operation longer than mine. I was intimidated by their success but didn't let that obstruct my desire to learn. After that experience, I realized that there would always be businesses that I can aspire to mimic and learn from their mistakes. I appreciate having those role models because their knowledge would help me improve myself. It's important to aspire to become better. When you self-improve, you engage in all aspects of the process because, in the end, you will be more successful.

Helping others is my biggest reward. As I tapped into my passion, I became self-aware and motivated to self-improve,

I noticed that my desire to help others was profound. Helping others is a selfless act. I don't help others looking for a return or need for them to reciprocate. It warms my heart to provide insight, knowledge, and use my expertise to assist others in any manner. I know what it feels like to feel hopeless and without support in your life. Having been diagnosed with post-traumatic stress disorder, I wanted help but didn't know how to ask or didn't want anyone to know my condition. I knew I needed help and when my symptoms exacerbated to a point where I felt depressed, felt worthless and hopeless, I had to ask for help. That changed my life. For the first time, I wasn't in control and needed someone else to help me get control of my life. I wasn't winning my war on PTSD. I knew in my darkest moments that I had to rely on someone else. I received that help, and it afforded me the opportunity to live a better life and to conquer my fears of being vulnerable and alone. When the chance presented itself for me to offer help to others, I jumped at it. I created an online resource for Veterans and their dependents to have when they feel alone and need help as they conquer their struggles with PTSD. I wanted to share the principles I used with others so that their lives would be better. My determination to create this resource was incredible. I felt a sense of urgency to share this information. I worked non-stop to gather my thoughts and set a deadline to promote the idea. I remember mentoring a gentleman in a PTSD crisis. It was remarkable to see his transformation from the beginning of our conversation to the end of it. I was elated to know that I could help transform a life on that day. I recall him stating that I had given him more insight into his coping mechanisms than anyone else. I was selfless during this encounter. I offered him my time, and my story as a means to help him relate and understand how his life can change as well. I was able to offer my experience, stayed engaged in his plight and helped him discover a plan for coping with his symptoms. At that moment, it wasn't about me but about how I could help him in his crisis. I was touched by his encounter and seeing how his life is changing in a positive way was rewarding.

Lastly, you have to decide who and what is worthy of your engagement. I had to decide that I was worth staying focused for my growth. My growth depended on me doing my 'check-ups' and re-engaging if I got side tracked. I knew that I needed supportive and positive people around me. I believe that like-minded people would help keep me engaged and would be worthy of my time. I realized a long time ago that not everyone is worthy of your time and energy. I had to decide who I would associate with and what activities would be beneficial to my self-improvement. I knew that I had to continue to work hard and believe in the end my hard work would pay off. I had to believe that if no one else believed in me that as long as I believed in myself, I would be okay. I had to leave people behind who didn't support my endeavors. Though initially painful, I had to power through that pain and decide that they weren't worthy of me investing a friendship or discussions of my plans. When you are really focused, those things that don't bring you positivity doesn't matter. Nothing matters but you being self-aware, always wanting to self-improve, connecting to your passion and helping others and only investing in things and people who are worthy. Becoming AT Peace and not in pieces requires your dedication, discovering your strength and knowing your weaknesses. You have to power through and remember that your journey entails you staying engaged and never losing sight of your destiny.

Chapter V: Acceptance

There are many things in our lives that we have to accept. But before we accept them, we must know what the definition of acceptance is. I believe if we had a clear understanding of the word acceptance, many of our trials and tribulations would not have occurred. Through my research, I have found many definitions of acceptance. The one that I favored the most is – Acceptance: It is the act of taking or receiving something offered, favorable reception, approval, and the action or process of being received as adequate or suitable. Being at peace with yourself requires that you understand what you are willing to accept and not accept. First, you must begin with knowing who you are in order to understand what you will allow to take place in your life. I know for me; it took a very long time for me to accept who I am. For many years, I identified myself as being the smart kid, the daughter, the military officer, the mother, and the list goes on and on. But that truly was not who I was. It took me having to finally sit down one day and ask myself who I was. I needed to discover who I was as a person looking for happiness without the influence of others and what they thought I needed. Once I discovered that, then I could accept who I was in that moment and in turn realize the things I would accept from other people.

I remember sitting on my couch, and it seemed like it took four hours for me to write the things that identified me. I recall the first thing I wrote was I'm a believer. Then I wrote I'm a giver, I'm humble, I'm unique, I'm a chooser and not the chosen, and finally, I'm a forgiver. As I am writing these things, I'm identifying some experiences I've had in the past that really molded me to be the person I am. I am a believer because had it not been for God in my spiritual upbringing a lot of my obstacles and conditions would have overtaken me and I would not be the success I am now. I am a giver because I believe it's better to give than to receive. My heart is happy when I am giving, and I give freely. I'm very humbled because I was taught not to boast and brag. I believe as easily as great things can come my way, they can also leave very quickly. I'm very grateful and gracious to people and things that have come my way because I never expected them to. I am unique because we are all different. At one point I wanted to look like a certain person or talk like a certain person or dress like a certain person until I woke up one day and realized I would never be that person, and I needed to accept who I was in the flesh. Being unique is great. That means there's no one else here like me. That means who I am is who I was intended to be. Now, I am a chooser and not the chosen because for many relationships in my life I was chosen instead of being the chooser.

My failures in relationships stemmed from not choosing my partners but allowing them to choose me. Because I was so grateful to be chosen, I allowed several situations to happen that I should not have, like paying bills that didn't belong to me and agreed to timeshares and new home constructions for the sake of saving a relationship. I remember being in this seven-month relationship with a gentleman that was considered a goddess externally. He was eye candy, tall and handsome. He was also a successful businessman or at least I thought so. I was captivated by who he was and presented myself to him in a way that allowed me to be chosen by him. What I mean by that is when I saw him around in the city, I knew his interests, and I knew his involvements. So I knew I could captivate his interests. By captivating his interests, I knew in time if he was available that he would choose me. After many phone calls and dinner dates, he did just that. It wasn't until that relationship failed and many hours of therapy that I understood what had happened. It was just not in this relationship that this was the common thread for me, but it was the commonality for many of my previous relationships. I was never taught that I had a voice or that I could choose my partner. I thought it was the reverse. It wasn't until my therapist asked, "Did you choose him?" I was baffled by her question and asked what do you mean did I choose him? She then replied, "Just because he chose you does not mean you had to choose him." It was the most awakening moment I've ever had in my life. A stranger, a therapist, someone who didn't know me as many people did, just said something so profound it shook me. I got excited. I said to her "I get to choose?" She said, "Yes and when you accept who you are and know what you want unconditionally, you will begin to understand the choosing and not being the chosen." She took this idea a little further and said let's list all of your relationships and you tell me how much of the choosing you did each of them. As we did the drill, we discovered that in my marriage, my ex-husband chose me. He saw in me great characteristics that exuded being a good wife. He asked for my hand in marriage and because he had chosen me I didn't take the time to assess if I had chosen him and I accepted his offer. Finding myself in that marriage, I discovered that in reality, he was not my chosen mate or someone I would choose to marry. That was a huge discovery for me sitting on her couch that day. I left home not understanding how important it was to know myself enough to know that I could choose. Lastly, I'm a forgiver. It took me years to finally realize that I was holding onto a lot of resentment and animosity because of the mistakes made. Not only the resentment for myself but also the resentment to others. I had to forgive myself for making the mistakes that I had made and forgiving those involved who didn't prepare me for life and its challenges.

There were many things in life that I had to accept. I had to accept that because of the divorce I was now going to be a single mother. I had to accept that having been deployed four times, later being diagnosed with posttraumatic stress disorder, and now I will be labeled a disabled veteran. I had to accept that being a survivor meant overcoming struggles every day that no one sees. I had to accept that innately, I am an advocate and motivator; and with that charge comes me encouraging and inspiring others through all my actions. I had to accept that being a CEO of my business meant making the hard executive decisions and trusting I'm making the right ones. I had to learn how to accept my successes as well as my failures. I had to learn that redemption was my true indication of accepting those failures. I believe when a mishap happens, or mistake happens you first must accept it and then decide how you're going to redeem yourself. It is not about how horrible you stumble or how hard you fall but how quickly and how determined you are to get back in the fight and begin again. This is one concept that I teach my daughters as they are growing into adulthood. They would complain about life not being fair and it being difficult to reach their goals because the support is not always there when needed. I would listen very closely to their thoughts, and afterwards, I would say, how long are you going to accept, allow or approve those consequences? They would look at me confused and question what I meant with the question. I would then say very supportively, how will you now move forward. I had to learn that you can sit and waddle in your own pity and complaint, or you can choose not to accept it and do something about it.

Acceptance is key to understanding because our actions are rooted in what we choose to do or choose not to do. It is key to know that what we accept or approve of in life will come with consequences to that decision. As we all know, the consequences could be great, or the consequences can be disastrous. As long as you understand and know what you're facing and are capable of accepting the repercussions, you will determine your growth and how you move forward in life. Acceptance is a solo decision. You have to determine for yourself what's important without interference from others. When you know yourself, you know your values, you know your morals, and you can accept the outcome of anything that comes your way. Without influences, you are now responsible for your fate. Only you will have to accept how things pan out.

Acceptance also means receiving and consenting to those things that you do not have control over. Now this definition is impactful. Being hopeful and wishful for a different outcome will not change the reality of what it is. For example, if it is snowing outside and you are hoping and wishing for a sunny day, you have to accept that is snowing. You can't change that reality, nor can you change that outcome. You are not in control of the weather so you cannot decide when it will be sunny or snowing. This example can also be used in everyday experiences. If you desire a higher paying job, you can search for higher-paying jobs, or you can choose to accept the one you have and stop complaining about it. Accepting reality is crucial to avoiding disasters because you are wanting and hoping for something different. Yes, there are many things in life that you can change that can help you accept certain experiences in life. You can change your hair color, and you can change the way you look with plastic surgery. Those things are all cosmetic changes and will never change the reality of who you truly are. This is hard for some people because you not only have to accept the great things about yourself but you also have to accept those awful things as well. Just as I listed those wonderful attributes that I related to my discovery, I also to accepted those things about myself that were not so great as well. I had to realize that I was not perfect, and I'm flawed. With that being said, I had to accept that I can be overbearing, curt, impatient, and a little judgmental. Now that I know those things I can then work to improve them. I discovered that being overbearing, curt, impatient and judgmental comes from the passion I have inside to help people better themselves. It is deeply rooted from my childhood days where I always wanted to be the helper and the Savior of anyone I met. So when I'm faced with the situation, and someone is asking for my help, my passion exhibits these flaws.

Every day you have to accept the choices and decisions that you make as well as the disappointments. I had to accept that my grandmother who was my hero and the matriarch of the family was dying. I always saw her as someone that would live forever. As unrealistic as that was, there was something about her that made her invincible. I remember the call I got from my father; he said we all needed to come home because my grandmother was fading quickly. Death was imminent. The drive to my mom's house was a very long one as I continued to my grandmothers, which was only 15 minutes away.

My grandmother's house was deeply rooted in the country. As I was driving, it was like slow motion, and I could count every tree that I passed. It seemed like that drive took forever. When I arrived, my father met me at the door. He expressed the alarming news that my hero was dying, and hospice was now there to provide her comfort. He wanted to warn me of what I would see entering her room. The very curvy and healthy woman that I remembered was not who I saw lying on her deathbed. Nothing that my father said could have prepared me for what I saw.

As I drew closer to the bed, I began to see flashbacks of her beautiful long gray hair that we would braid upon her request. I saw her smile; I remembered her feisty voice and the little pearls of wisdom she would give all of us. I'm afraid of what was lying in the bed, lifeless and skeletal, so my memories calmed and soothed me. I curled up in the bed next to her and snuggled with her for a while. I recall her slow, shallow breathing and periods of apnea. In those moments, I would stroke her hand and say I'm here, then she would continue her rhythmic breathing. I stroked her hair, her face, and her hands as if I was embedding her blueprint into my brain. This was the woman who told me at a very young age that I would succeed and that I had a gift, and the world would know my name. Though feeble, I could still hear her strong heartbeat. While lying next to her, I would feel a twitch or a slight movement in her fingers as if she wanted to squeeze my hands. This was a bittersweet moment because though we said nothing to each other, I could feel that she felt my presence, and I could definitely feel her presence as well. I recall my father knocking on the door and requesting that I come out and let her sleep. I kissed her forehead, said "I love you" and thanked her for her wisdom and her belief in me, and I told her that I would make her proud. Several days after this encounter, my hero died, and it was my first experience on how to accept and cope with death. I knew that I had to move forward with my life. Her memories are still near and dear to my heart, and though I was disappointed by her demise, I grew to know that just like death there are occurrences in your life that you must accept. I took this lesson to be my model for acceptance. The serenity prayer says: God grant me the serenity to accept the things I cannot change, the courage to change the things I can, and the wisdom to know the difference. This prayer changed my life and gave me comfort in the decisions and outcomes that have happened in my life. I had to learn to accept what I could bear, contain, improve, defend, and let go. I matured enormously once I understood my role in accepting those particulars that would make me happy. I knew my happiness depended on me speaking my truth and accepting the consequences that followed.

Powering through my pain of acceptance meant that I not only had to accept me, my mishaps, my disappointments and my diagnosis of PTSD but any realities that I was faced with at that time. When you're powering through acceptance, remember that you have to be realistic, and you have to be accepting of the consequences following your decision. Not that the pain will be less, but you have a greater understanding of your decision and become more compelled to accept the outcome. Remember to be at peace you have to power through the pain of acceptance. Accepting yourself is important, allowing time for redemption, getting back up, forgiving yourself, and being available to accept the next challenge is imperative.

Chapter VI: Courage

Courage is defined as the ability to do something that frightens you or strength in the face of pain or grief. In order to be at peace, you have to have the courage to go through all the previous steps and remain strong and not turn back. Being courageous means you have to cast aside fear and doubt and just know and believe you will complete the task at hand. I believe we are all courageous, but it is fear that prevents us from really overcoming those things that utter self-doubt and disbelief into our consciousness. I think the most beautiful thing in life is seeing a baby attempt to walk.

When it was time for my daughters to take their first step, the days before they would crawl to the sofa, bring themselves up onto their feet and then shuffle around the sofa. We had a coffee table that was in front of the sofa and after many hours of them shuffling around the sofa table; they decided they would try to get their balance and reach for the coffee table. At that moment they were courageous. They didn't think about the, what if's; they just went for it. Once one did it, the other followed. They would chuckle because now they had discovered a new game, moving from sofa to the coffee table. After doing this for several days and extending their reach, the day came that they would take their first step. I remember holding my breath because Anita was up. She was the first one up at bat. Their father and I knew that they were ready to take their first steps. So we stood Anita up a few steps away from the coffee table. She stood there, and she rocked a little bit until she got her balance, then she took her first step and stopped. Then she took her next step, got her balance, then she stopped. She stretched out her hands to see how close she was to the coffee table. She saw that she was real close, so she decided to take more steps to get to the coffee table. Two more steps and she was there. We all clapped and cheered, she was smiling and so excited. Ashley had witnessed what Anita had done, and Ashley was up next. We stood Ashley in the exact same spot we had stood Anita. Ashley took her first step, then her second step, then her third and final step to the table. Ashley saw from Anita's experience that as long as she stayed balanced on her feet, she could make it to the table. We all cheered, laughed and were excited. From then on we would see them take more steps, and before we knew it, they were no longer crawling but walking and running. This is an excellent example of how we are all courageous. Even in doubt, we can overcome it and still have the courage to complete a mission. That example is also enlightenment on how we all have the innate courage to do whatever we put our minds to.

There are many life experiences for which I had to connect to my inner strength to overcome. I had to stand in my truth in knowing that my status was no longer married with children but a single mother of twin daughters. That took a while for me to be courageous enough to say that because of the stigma of being a single mother. Immediately when someone hears of a single mother, the thought is that she is a woman who is struggling because she has kids and nobody will want her. I had to be courageous enough to stand in my truth in knowing that I might be single for a while. I had to be okay with my status and not be afraid of what would or could come because of it. Actually, I felt courageous being single because I had been married for nine years. Leaving a marriage and now entering singlehood to some may be a difficult transition. But for me, I wasn't afraid nor did I run from the experience.

When you are courageous, you run towards obstacles and don't look back. While teaching my daughters how to drive, I gave them a great analogy of why cars have rearview mirrors. I said to them "notice that the rearview mirror is smaller than your front window." The reason for that is because even in life those things in the rear of you, behind you, your past, that Mirror is intended for you to get a glimpse to make sure you recall and not duplicate those experiences but leave them in the past. You want to always be aware of who and what is behind you. That mirror is not intended for you to look at it for a long period of time. However, your front window is much larger. It is much larger because you can now view everything that's in front of you. The front window is your future. That's what you are driving towards. It's bigger because your life is ever evolving and this big window allows you to embrace all those experiences in your future.

It is pretty ironic that when I think of courage, I think of the many talks my daughters and I would have about my deployment and how I survived them all. Sometimes circumstances around you can put fear into your mind and heart. I think it was the fear of the unknown going to combat the first time that challenged how courageous I was. Going to the briefings and hearing others recall their disappointment did nothing for me as far as preparation. It wasn't until I arrived at my first deployment that I really began to understand that I would have to be courageous in order to get back home safely. We were told of the different injuries we would see as nurses in a combat hospital, but seeing and believing were different. After seeing all the different types of amputations, burns, gunshot wounds, I was courageous to keep it together and help heal the soldiers. There was one incident that tested my courage....

That Day......

Lying in bed feeling vulnerable and fearless, I knew this day was different. I slept about five hours, which is really great considering the constant rush of incoming rockets while under attack both day and night. My cell phone buzzed signaling an incoming text from my commander. I jumped up because my commander had never texted before so I immediately knew this was not good. I read the disheartening text requesting that I report immediately to the emergency room and not to report to the CASF because it was bombed and was unsafe at this time. I knew this day would come. Each day I would walk to the CASF, I always felt like our facility was too open for the enemy to attack us at any time. I remember asking that question during orientation from the outgoing commander and the response was we hadn't been hit yet. That was definitely reassuring. Though surrounded by cement barricades, the CASF was on the flight line, open to anyone wanting to attack us. So, hearing from my commander that this had indeed happened was like an omen that I felt deep in my heart had come true. I rushed to get dressed in a hyper-vigilant state of mind because usually at that time of the day attacks were frequent. Walking along to the emergency room, every step seemed to have taken me a step away from the ER instead of a step closer. That was the longest walk of my life. My heart was racing, my M9 was ready to fire, my body armor was snug, and my helmet was strapped and secure. Walking through the maze of multiple tents, I finally got to the gate of the ER. Tonight it seemed more illuminated, and an eerie feeling came across my body before entering. I paused and said a prayer because I didn't know the chaos I was going to see when those doors opened. I opened my eyes and in front of me were some of my enlisted airmen walking towards me. In their eyes, I saw fear, anger, and fright. Many were crying and unable to speak. Everything was moving so fast. What was happening? What's going on? I was standing there, and the world was spinning around me. I was frozen, feet anchored to the floor. I took a deep breath and went inside composed and poised because everyone was expecting me to be. I saw my commander and he walked over, and he told me the details of the attack.

The Afghans' rocket landed on our generator behind our tent, exploding it sent shrapnel through the tent injuring one of our soldiers. Shrapnel hit the airman and injured his leg and scalp. He would be going to emergency surgery, and the commander wanted everyone there for support, accountability, and debrief. I then went over to the airmen in the bay of the ER to console and comforted him. He was elated that we were all there. He was a young airman who never had surgery before and here he is in a combat zone without his wife and kids and about to have major surgery. The chaplain was there, and we all prayed for him, and he went off to surgery. Now it was time to check on the emotional, psychological and physical state of the rest of the squadron. Several airmen who were present during the attack were still shaken, and Mental Health officers were there to support them. Others needed to hear that reassurance from me that they would return home safely to their families back in the US. How could I reassure them of this when I wasn't even sure I was going to make it back? I was already playing Russian Roulette because this was my fourth deployment. I needed to say something because we had to get back to work. An attack doesn't stop the mission. It put the mission on hold but the mission must carry on. Confused and angry myself, I had to put aside my feelings to step up and be the officer I was conditioned to be.

I spoke with each airman offering my support and relaying the message that we can't focus on the "what-ifs" out here. We have to live each day alert, aware, and ready for anything. There was absolutely nothing any of them could have done to stop the attack. We are in a war zone. This is what happens. For many of them, this was their first deployment, and some of the nurses had been in the military less than four years. Normally our night shift crew is jovial, fun and we would do silly things to keep us up and prepare for our mission. It was one of the best crews I've ever worked with in all my deployments. But tonight, we all worked in utter disbelief, minimal talking, and in slow motion. Assignments were given, and everyone was on task. Once the mission was complete and our CASF was cleared by security and was safe, we all went back to our CASF sent to see the aftermath of the attack.

Prior to this night, all I had ever seen was the wounded soldiers from the battlefield and nursed their wounds. But tonight, I got to see what hate and evil looked like. Approaching the nearly destroyed CASF, you could still smell the smoke and see the burnt areas of the tent. Going inside, I saw the mass destruction. Shrapnel had pierced through the tent, and you could see the moonlight peeking in the holes of the tent. The blast from the impact had punctured holes through the back door. The door was wooden and was the only solid attachment to the tent. We had no electricity, so I used my flashlight to see inside. Cabinets, books, aluminum chairs, even our helmets were destroyed by the shrapnel. I remember trying to replay in my head what happened in that exact moment. *1. The rocket hit the generator. 2. Everyone heard the noise and took cover. 3. There is yelling and screaming telling everyone to get down and take cover. 4. The sound of metal shrapnel is swarming into the tent like bees on a hive. 5. The yell for help as the soldiers notice that he was hit. 6. The team is crawling over to the airman to provide first aid until the attack was over. 7. Everyone thinking that we will get hit again. 8. How are we going to get out of here? 9. Am I going to die today?*

Collecting my thoughts and emotions, I saw what hate looked like. In that tent without lights, surrounded by holes in the walls and door, inside in total disarray, I could smell evil. At that moment, I felt that these actions were unexplainable, unwarranted, destructive, fearful and scary. I felt myself suffocating from the intense psychological toll this moment was taking on me. I had to get out to there. I worked my way through the tent reminiscing on how it looked before the attack and how it looked now. Each breath is getting harder and harder. Finally, outside this debacle, I had walked to the front of the CASF, which was several feet from the flight line. There was no movement. No noise or sounds. The sky was dark, and I could see very small glittering dots in the sky like fireflies. I tried to scream, but no sound would come out. I tried to cry, but no tears would fall. I tried to speak, but no words would form. I just stood there in the open like the CASF, open to be destroyed and killed. I felt hopeless, alone, bitter, and punctured like the walls of the tent.

The enemy had done this to me. The Afghans had violated not only our space but our security. I remember looking up towards the heavens and throwing up my middle fingers and saying, "Screw you Afghanistan!" I heard my voice and continued saying "you will not break me, and I'm leaving this place alive, watch me!" This attack now became personal. It was me against the Afghans. I laugh at it now because of what was I going to do. I'm an army of one against an army of many. At that time, I needed something to get me through that night. I had to be strong for those airmen looking up to me, and I had to be strong so I could survive mentally what just happened. I am Captain Jackson, Superwoman with

Superpowers to strike the enemy down with one blow. Who was I kidding? But telling myself that worked because we finished the mission that night. When morning came and we could see the devastation in the daylight, man what a mess. The CASF looked destroyed, and it did not look like it could be repaired. We all knew that this tent would need to come down, and we would be relocated. The day shift came in, and turnover was given to them. The day shift crew looked tired, still shaken by the events of the day before, but courageous. I mentioned to them all before leaving how proud I was of them for getting through that event and that if they needed to talk that I would make myself available.

One nurse pulled me aside and asked how I did three prior deployments under this pressure. I said I never focused on the what if's but lived each day on task to complete each mission assigned. I told her to remember why she was there. We were there to support the wounded soldiers and get them back home to their families. Focusing on anything else would derail her and allow her to be vulnerable and weak when the enemy attacked. She nodded to acknowledge what I said, but I knew in her heart she was contemplating the whys, what ifs, coulda, woulda and shoulda's. That was okay. She would process what she needed in her own time. I walked away from the CASF looking at the huge snow capped mountains on the opposite side of the flight line wondering how something so beautiful could be the hidden location for the cowards that wanted to kill us. I walked to my room that morning instead of getting a ride to the dorms. I kept repeating the Lords Prayers until I got to my room. I sat on the floor after taking off my body armor, helmet and backpack, M9, and M9 holster. I couldn't hold it inside anymore; I cried and this time, tears came. I screamed and yelled, and I could hear the sound. The moment lasted for about a minute, then I gathered my shower caddy, my PT gear and went to shower off the sadness from the last 16 hours. It's a new day. A new beginning. Another day to be thankful that I was alive. Another day closer to leaving and getting home.

The day after......

The next day the mood was different. No one knew what the day would bring. We went on doing what we normally did trying to forget the events of the night before. I could see in their eyes how scared and uncertain they felt. No one talked about what happened. We had a new mission which involved sending out more patients to Germany for further intervention. Everyone worked hard as if work would erase how they felt. Then at 0200 the attack siren goes off, we had thrown ourselves onto the floor, covered our heads and waited a few seconds to ensure shrapnel wasn't landing and piercing our bodies. I looked around and yelled, "Is everyone Okay?" I heard all the voices say "yes ma'am." We all then sprinted to the cement bunker next to the tent. Inside the bunker everyone was quiet. We could hear the gunshots fire across the bunker. The attack went on for several minutes. No one knew what would happen. Is this the day that we would die?

There is nowhere to go in the bunker. I had to take charge. I tried to console them knowing that I didn't have an answer. This was the safest place we could be. As we heard the gunshots ricochet off the bunker, many begin to cry. I could feel their thoughts. Wondering if today was the day that they would lose their lives. Thinking about their families, kids, loved ones back home, to be circling in their minds. I too was scared and afraid. I thought of my daughters and their futures. The thought of how devastating it would be to know that their mother had died in combat. At that moment, I began to pray. I prayed to God that we would be safe and make it through that attack safely. Though I prayed and prayed and prayed something deep down inside told me that today could be the day. In the darkness of the bunker, you could hear subtle movements. Everyone tried to remain quiet hoping that the quietness will cease the gunfire. Then we heard a rocket pass the bunker. The sound of that rocket overhead with the whistling sound like the wind sent the message that death was imminent. I heard the rocket land. It did not detonate. That's never a good sign. But for the moment, it gave me peace and solace knowing that no one was hurt. We sat in that bunker, and it seemed like hours passed, hoping the attack would end soon. How long could it go on like this? How many more attacks could we endure? We were only halfway through this deployment, so this attack made us question if we would make it.

Then suddenly, the alarm signaled that we were in the clear. I heard my troops breathe. They were relieved to have known that they had survived. They began to speak as if these were their first words they've ever spoken. I can now see their eyes in the bunker. We all gathered our items that we brought in with us, and walked out, and we could smell the smoke from the attack. We all looked around wondering who got hit. Thank God it wasn't us again. Our building was still standing. We entered the tent knowing that we had to complete a mission. We all separated into our groups, got our assignments for the night, and went on our way. Again no one talked about the events of what we just endured. We were grateful to be alive. Another day, another minute, another hour and we were still alive.

Being courageous can come in many different forms and fashions. As I look back over my life, I have many examples of being courageous. I had to be courageous to leave home at 17 years old and know that I was equipped to handle the world. I could not allow fear to keep me in a marriage that was unfulfilling and unhealthy. I could not allow fear to prevent me from being the best mother I can be while also being a soldier in the military. I had to be brave enough to rid myself of anyone who wasn't supportive or envious of my success. I had to be brave enough to stand in my truth and know that I didn't have to compare myself to others. I had to believe that I was good enough and that my journey would lead me to happiness. Being courageous also means sometimes you have to be bold and spontaneous. Sometimes you have to be fearless.

When I decided to start my own business as a nurse consultant and CEO of Jackson and Associates, I had to be courageous. I've never been an entrepreneur before. I knew I wanted to create a business which would leave a legacy behind for my daughters. I had no examples to follow in my family of anyone that were entrepreneurs. This was a new endeavor which required me to be brave and to be firm in my decision. I did the necessary research, and I did the necessary preparation in order to be ready to embark on being a business person. I had not gone to school to learn business nor did I know the proper procedures or protocols to start a business. I sought after mentors and other successful business people who could guide me along the way. I knew I had a great idea for a business, but I had to bring that idea to fruition in order to make it successful. It took me several months to tell people that I was now a CEO because I was afraid that if it had failed, I would be devastated. I waited until after I got my first paid client before announcing that I had opened my own business.

I remember shaking in my boots when I went to do the interview for the case and speaking with the attorney about what I could offer them. I left the office knowing that he was not going to give me the case. Several days had passed, and I got an email stating that they were impressed with my presentation and wanted me to be a part of their team on the case. I was totally elated and believed nothing could stop me. Of course, as a business person, there's going to be pitfalls and mishaps along the way. I receive them as lessons learned and later discovered that every successful business owner has the same misfortunes along the way. But it was courage and bravery that kept me wanting to learn more and pursue other clients. I could have easily curled up in a ball and become invisible, but instead, I chose to push through in the hopes to be an inspiration to others.

So what happens when you're not courageous or brave? How do you not let fear paralyze you in order for you to reach your goals in life? What I've learned is that you have to learn to encourage yourself. You have to support yourself. I believe in supporting everybody that I come in contact with. But what I've found is while I'm someone else's cheerleader, I didn't have someone in my corner cheering me on. It's very draining when you are uplifting and encouraging others, but no one is there to encourage you. So instead of being angry and upset about not receiving the same support when fear comes, I learned to speak words of affirmation to myself in order to keep me brave and courageous. I would say to myself: I AM awesome, I AM brave, I AM beautiful, I AM great. I noticed that when I said these words of affirmation not only out loud but believed them internally, that I no longer needed anyone to encourage and inspire me. I then became my own cheerleader. Sometimes being courageous means you have to stand alone, and you have to support yourself. There's absolutely nothing wrong with it. So the next time you feel like you have no support or are uninspired, take a moment to find your positive words of affirmation and speak them to yourself. It may take a couple of tries in order for you to believe what you speak but when you do, you will find that your entire demeanor and outlook on life will change. Now that's being courageous.

I had to be courageous about my diagnosis of posttraumatic stress disorder. I had been diagnosed for several years before announcing to the world that I indeed was coping with my symptoms with PTSD. I didn't want the stigma or the isolation or the scrutiny that usually comes with that diagnosis. It wasn't until I realized that my coping could help someone else. I left home not understanding how important it was to know myself enough to know that I could choose. At first, I didn't want the world to know and have my life dissected and scrutinized. I didn't want them to see the vulnerabilities that came with me exposing my depression, isolation, loneliness, and hopelessness.

It wasn't until I was given the opportunity to be featured in Prevention magazine and exposing my experience that I realized my story was not only going to help me but was going to help those across the world that I couldn't touch personally. I remember the reporter calling and she began asking some real personal questions. She could hear me get silent on the phone, and she said you're going to help so many people by telling your story. She continued to say; please feel free to open up your heart and discuss your experience because your bravery is going to impact so many lives. After hearing her say those words, I became more open and began to let all the emotions out. I felt cleansed because I had not told anyone of my battle at all. Trusting a stranger with my story and believing that it will impact lives that I could not touch personally was the most courageous thing I've ever done in my life. I'm glad I did it. Sometimes you have to do things that are uncomfortable to be courageous. The impact I was going to have on people's lives was more important than me being uncomfortable. When I reflect on that experience, I get so much joy and peace because I know deep down inside that if I can do that, I can do anything.

As you can see, I had to power through the pain of being fearful many times in my life. I was once told that fear is false evidence appearing real. That is so true. The next time you encounter fear remember that fear is false. Fear is not a true experience. Don't be afraid to tackle that next endeavor that you were afraid of. Be courageous in everything that you do. Don't allow fear to cripple you. Fear is an imitation of a courageous outcome, but you have to be willing to show up and face fear in the face. When you power through the pain of fear, don't forget that your words of affirmation will help encourage you. If you have cheerleaders in your corner great but if not, you know how to encourage yourself. Being courageous means you are unstoppable. Being courageous means you have the ability to conquer the world. Have faith and know that you are strong and brave. The footprint of your life called destiny awaits you, and you cannot allow fear to hinder your success.

Chapter VII: Empower

These principles that I have guided you through this far: acknowledgment, transition, perseverance, engage, acceptance, and courage, have all built up to this one word: empower. When you empower someone, it means to give confidence or strength to something, often by enabling them to increase their control over their own life or situation. No matter what you endure or face in life, you have to feel confident and have an inner most strength to overcome those obstacles. No one can do it for you. You have to believe in yourself.

Many times we want to lean on others to feel empowered. Feeling empowered has to come from within. I didn't understand this concept until my recent diagnosis of posttraumatic stress disorder. I knew what the symptoms looked like for I had taken care of many soldiers with PTSD. I was confident that I could take care of the soldiers, but I wasn't confident that I could take care of myself. It wasn't until I asked for help that I realized that help was available for me. Because my symptoms didn't appear like many others symptoms, I didn't believe my PTSD required or needed attention. It wasn't until I was sitting at home alone and began recalling many experiences from my multiple deployments that I knew I was in trouble. So many times before I was in control of my life and did the things I needed to do to be successful. However, this time, I was not in control. I didn't have the strength at that time to cope and or deal with my diagnosis. It wasn't until I got the necessary tools and was giving multiple coping strategies that I got my confidence back. I began feeling strengthened and believed that I could once again have control of my life. That was empowerment. I went through the necessary steps in order to ensure I gained control.

1. *I was aware of my diagnosis.*
2. *I realized I needed help.*

3. *I obtained help.*
4. *I was given strategies.*
5. *I implemented the strategies.*
6. *And then gained my confidence back.*

These are the necessary steps that you have to take in order to feel empowered in your life. It doesn't matter what the consequence or the situation; it matters what you do in order to gain your strength and control.

When I feel empowered, I feel like I'm on top of the world. I feel like I am unstoppable, I'm in control, I'm at the top of my game, and nothing and no one can deter me. That's how I want you to feel working through these principles. This is where we were going to put the equation, but I think using all the principles in the equation will make the equation too long. How about this formula:

$$\underline{\text{Acknowledge + Perseverance = Empowerment}}$$
$$\text{AT PEACE}$$

Apply these principles to every aspect of your life and you feel empowered. Not only did I apply these principles to my diagnosis of posttraumatic stress disorder, but I also applied it to me being a successful business person, being a single parent, overcoming financial ruins, surviving deployments, unsuccessful relationships, and being a mentor to my daughters. I believe the hardest principle is the acknowledgment. And that's why I made that principle first. You can't move forward in any situation until you acknowledge that there is a situation that you must deal with. I realize that in therapy when the therapist asked me to acknowledge my behavior, it was very difficult for me to do. Because acknowledging it meant that I had to accept that behavior, good or bad. And oftentimes it was a behavior that I wasn't proud of. However, by accepting the behavior, I could then understand why I behaved that way and could decide how to transition from doing that behavior again. This was pivotal for me because often times we do what's comfortable and our norm. So transitioning allowed me to go outside my norm, I knew if I continued the process that the behavior would be different. Once I worked through the remaining principles, I understood the need to change my behavior because I was willing to do so and confident that I could, I felt empowered. Again these principles can be applied to many circumstances in your life. The goal is to reach that point that you can feel empowered and in control.

At certain stages of working through the principles, it can become difficult. There will be times where you don't want to acknowledge, and you don't want to transition. You are too tired to persevere, you don't want to be engaged, you don't want to accept, and you're not trying to be courageous, but if you don't, then you won't be empowered. It all goes back to what I mentioned my personal trainer would say to me when I wanted to quit, "How bad do you want it?" Change is not easy. Change is a voluntary action for which you can choose to change or not change. You have to decide how bad you want it.

Sometimes when you can't find within you the ability to feel empowered, you may have to find a role model to pattern after. I reflect on many of the soldiers that I had the pleasure of taking care of and analyzed how strong they are to get through their obstacles each day, particularly the soldiers who had amputations. Many times we get bogged down in our daily lives and think our challenges are difficult and unbearable. But when you see how an amputee gets through his/her day, it makes your challenges look very trivial. Imagine not having both of your legs and you are now bound to a wheelchair or having to rely on your prosthetics in order to walk. Imagine your life being changed physically where you can no longer do your daily tasks without asking for help or having to rely on a piece of equipment to get things done. Seeing amputees go about their daily lives with motivation and strength have empowered me. Seeing amputee's complete marathons, powerlifting competitions, CrossFit workouts of the day, and walk proudly with their heads high, give me that extra push to move to my challenges. You think our life and your burdens are difficult, reflect on others who are worse off than you. Reflect on situations that could have broken your spirit and your emotions but didn't. When you conquered the things that you thought you could not complete, you should feel empowered. Any time you succeed at a task that you put your mind to, no matter how long it takes you to complete, you should feel empowered. Just like an amputee had to find the inner strength to take that first step with his prosthetic, you have to find that first step to conquering your fears. What I've discovered is fear will hinder you from being the best person you can be. When fear steps in, it will make you stand still and not move forward towards your destiny. I command that you not let fear hold you hostage like a prisoner but instead feel empowered to break through and claim victory over your life.

When you power through your pains, you have no other choice but to feel empowered. As you work through the principles, and you become aware of the changes, you know that you are moving towards empowerment. Many times as I moved towards empowerment, with each step I get closer to success, I feel joy and happiness in my spirit. I feel like I can run a marathon and win a gold medal at the Olympics. My mind is clear, my focus is unwavered, and my determination leads me to the finish line. Nothing and no one will stop me. I pray and hope that you too can be AT PEACE with yourself, and your life's journey will bring you prosperity and happiness. No matter what comes your way remember to acknowledge, transition, persevere, engage, accept, be courageous, and feel empowered.

Chapter VII Journal Pages

Chapter VIII: Conclusion

Don't quit!

The purpose of this book is to truly help you be At Peace and Not in Pieces. It's natural that we all go through obstacles in life, but it is how you overcome those obstacles that will bring you peace. Peace not only in your heart but also in your body and soul. Being at peace does not mean that you have to forget a circumstance or situation. Being at peace means that you accept and are willing to move forward through that circumstance in that situation. Oftentimes we get stuck in that pit of an unfortunate situation and don't have the proper tools in order to pull ourselves out of the quicksand. The principles detailed in this book will guide you as you search for a way out. I wish I had these tools when I was experiencing my divorce, parenting my twin daughters alone, facing all the trials and deployments, financial ruins, and all the mishaps that my journey has brought me. It's funny when we reflect on our lives and our mistakes, one of the first things we all say is "had I known that I would've done it differently." Hopefully, after reading this book, you will no longer have to say those words.

I believe the most precious and peaceful thing to watch is a baby sleeping. They have not conceptualized the world yet so what are they dreaming about? What are their thoughts while they are sleeping that makes them want to smile while sleeping? Wouldn't it be great to know that one thing so that we can enter into our daily rituals with complete peace and tranquility? Waking up feeling too blessed to be stressed, or a sense of positivity that no one can change would be outstanding. Imagine a world where there is nothing but joy and hope; a world that is free from crime, hurt, and pain. What a wonderful life we would all have! Unfortunately, a life filled with roses, daisies, hummingbirds and sunflowers is not a life that we live. Powering through your pain will allow you to get there. Processing all of the principles will help you get there.

One of the many objectives I wanted to capture in this book is to ensure it was relatable to readers who are suffering not only from combat stress and posttraumatic stress disorder from deployments; but also to other fallen heroes suffering in silence. This includes so many individuals like first responders, firefighters, police officers, rape victims, sexual assault victims, and the list goes on and on. This book is not specific to one group of people. It's intended to touch the hearts of anyone who has challenges and is looking for a resource to overcome them. These principles can be taught to young girls searching for their identity and self-esteem. These principles can be taught to prisoners behind bars who need to accept their crimes and punishments for their wrongdoing. These principles can be taught to single parents wanting to be the best parents they can be and raise successful and respectful children. So as you can see, At Peace Not In Pieces can be a guide to help everyone.

One of my favorite quotes is from Dr. Martin Luther King Jr. He stated that "The ultimate measure of a man is not where he stands in moments of comfort and convenience, but where he stands at times of challenge and controversy." How you stand and face your challenges and controversies will determine how your morals and character are shaped. I was taught that when times get hard and tough, you have to dig in your heels, keep fighting and refuse to be knocked down. I recall a friend who said to me that she was so tired of swinging because life kept throwing her more punches and she wanted to give up. I reminded her that it was her willpower that kept her swinging. That meant she was a fighter, a survivor, and an overcomer. I told her to continue to swing until she couldn't swing anymore. Even when she didn't have the strength to swing one last time, she remembered that she had feet and could kick. I wanted her to know that there were other ways to attack a challenge besides the one she knew. Hopefully, all my readers will understand that concept as well. Sometimes life sucks. It's not about how you are in that moment of pain, sorrow, and unhappiness but how you rebound from it. Wounds will heal. Broken bones will mend. Scars will scab over and slough off.

We are stronger than we know, but we have to tap into our inner strength and become Hercules, Wonder Woman, or even the Incredible Hulk. All of these cartoon characters were heroes because no matter what enemy they faced they would always win the battle. What cartoon character will you be as you power through your pain?

I wrote this book because I wanted to share with the world my experiences and offer my journey and tools as a way to motivate, inspire and encourage every reader. I wanted to be as transparent and as genuine as possible as a form of gratitude to the universe for sparing my life on the battlefields and keeping my mind intact as I endure my struggles of PTSD. I didn't choose my life; it was chosen for me. There's absolutely nothing I would undo about my life at this point. Every aspect of my life prepared me to be At Peace, Not in Pieces. Had I not had my heart broken, I would not know what true love is. Had I not hit rock bottom with my finances, I would not understand the true meaning of financial freedom and security. Had I not gone to war, I would not have known how strong my faith was and how much my spirituality really means to me. What I learned writing this book, is that there are absolutely no excuses to accomplishing and completing tasks and goals. None! The only person that will hold you back from success is yourself. The journey of writing this book has allowed me to see that saying "I can't" was only an excuse. Saying can't or I don't think I will, or I'm not sure were only barricades that I chose to hide behind while suppressing all my talents that have been gifted to me. Never again. So I challenge you after reading this book to do something that you thought you couldn't do. Find that one thing that you have excused or suppressed because you were afraid to attempt it or didn't have the courage to explore it, go for it and JUST DO IT! Life is too short to live your life on dreams deferred or coulda's, shoulda's, woulda's.

Have you ever imagined being something you never thought you could be? How fantastic would that be! I never imagined that I would be an author, but here I am. I never imagined that I would be a business owner, but here I am. I never imagined that I would be a speaker in front of hundreds of people, but here I am.

One of the greatest lines from the movie and the book "The Help" was when the main character taught the little girl at the end three things: she was smart, she was kind, and she was important. After reading this book I hope that you feel "powerful," rock solid in who you are and sure about where you want to go. I hope that you feel "liberated," unshackled by all your hurts, pains, and mishaps; and lastly, "empowered," totally emancipated to be your best self that you can be and unwilling to be defeated. I discovered that there was greatness inside of me that I had never known. It was when I felt powerful, liberated, and empowered that I could stand in my greatness. The result of this discovery was being At Peace and being capable of powering through my pain.

I'm very humbled that you chose to read this book. My hope is that you live a better life with hope, joy, and happiness. Sharing my journey was a way for me to impact the lives of others. I believe I've had so many people impact my life along the way that it was my duty to do the same. My true believers that knew my capabilities even before I could see them, I'm forever indebted. This book is about living life to the fullest without excuses, shame, or regrets. Time waits for no one, and I wouldn't want anyone to waste time getting to their destiny if I can provide the tools to assist. It is my desire that you get to your destiny sooner than later because the greatness that lives inside of you can change the world.

Chapter VIII Journal Pages

About the Author

Captain Cherissa Jackson is a retired Air Force Nurse with 14 years of nursing experience.   She has served 23 years and survived 4 deployments – 3 to combat hospitals. She is a SHERO United Ambassador and a Hall of Famer for her efforts to help women veterans. Her passion to motivate, inspire and encourage has led her to be an advocate for Post-Traumatic Stress soldiers and their families.

In 2015, Captain Jackson launched PTSfaces, a global platform that brings awareness to the treatment and the treatment options for PTS Veterans. This online one stop shop provides support groups, partnerships, medial teams, webinars, survival stories, and other resources to any veterans looking for support and assistance with coping with PTS.

 PTSFaces was created from Captain Jackson's own experiences as a survivor of PTSD and the stories of other Veterans challenged with their condition. Four tours of duty in some of the worst war zones required Captain Jackson to compartmentalize her emotions. Re-bandaging charred bodies as she inhaled the smell of burned skin and watching injured soldiers with amputated limbs emerge from helicopters were a part of her daily work. After the bombing in Afghanistan of her building in 2011, which caused her to live in fear for six months, Captain Jackson ultimately retired. When she returned, she was haunted by the memories from her deployments and suffered from increased anxiety. Soon after, Captain Jackson was diagnosed with PTSD. With a few months on prescribed medication, continued exercise, and her will to conquer PTSD, Captain Jackson stands today as a PTS Survivor ready to help her fellow Veterans combat PTSD.

Passionate about helping others and determined to make a difference, helping other war veterans overcome the challenge and the stigma of PTSD has become Cherissa Jackson's new legacy and mission.

Captain Jackson is also the CEO of Jackson & Associates Legal Nurse Consultants and is a proud mother of 2 beautiful twin daughters.

Captain Jackson has been featured various media outlets including Forbes, Prevention Magazine, The Washington Post, The Daily Record, and the Examiner.